A SEASON TILL

Spring

A SEASON TILL Spring

J. B. PERRY

BEACON HILL PRESS OF KANSAS CITY
KANSAS CITY, MISSOURI

ISBN: 083-411-3937

Printed in the
United States of America

Cover Design: Royce Ratcliff
Cover Illustration: Keith Alexander

10 9 8 7 6 5 4 3 2 1

For
Bud, Lois, and Ken
and
Jim, Gertie, Judy, and Rex—
who believed in us

1

·····

*T*HE GLARE OF TOO MANY overhead lights cast harsh shadows in the nearly deserted airport. Intermittently, a loudspeaker droned flight information in the background. Jessica Sterling stood wearily with a small line of other late-night travelers waiting to check her bags. The calamity of the last 12 hours had etched itself deeply into her countenance. She stared vacantly at the ticket jacket in her hand.

The large suitcase on the floor beside Jessie looked too heavy for her slender frame, but when her turn came, she easily lifted it to the baggage platform at the check-in counter.

"Flight number?" the gray-haired ticket agent asked without taking his eyes from the computer screen.

"I'm not sure." Jessie's dark hair fell softly around her face as she fumbled with her ticket. "It's the 10:49 flight from Long Beach to Boston."

The older man lifted his eyes from his work impatiently and peered over the rim of his glasses. His gaze softened as he met Jessie's swollen and bloodshot eyes. Embarrassed, Jessie turned her face away from his pity.

"I'll take care of it, Miss," the agent said gruffly. "Sit in the waiting area, and I'll bring your ticket to you in a moment."

Jessie gratefully made her way to the row of black chairs in the boarding area. Her steps echoed hollowly on the parquet floor. Just as she was about to sit down she heard her name.

"Jessie! Hey, Jessie!" The voice came from the far end of the terminal. Even at that distance Jessie recognized it immediately. Brad. Still in his hospital greens, the stethoscope he wore around his neck bounced crazily as he ran toward her.

Panting from the long run, he pulled her into his arms. "I just got your message," he said between breaths. "Jessie, I'm so sorry."

He held her tightly and stroked her hair. Jessie didn't have the emotional energy to return his embrace. She stood quietly, arms at her sides, letting him hold her, finding a small measure of comfort in his touch.

"They're dead, Brad," she whispered finally. "Both of them."

He tilted her face toward his. How lovely she was—even now when her usually vibrant green eyes were clouded with sorrow. Tall and dark skinned, Jessie was the kind of woman who drew attention in crowds. She carried herself with grace and self-assurance, yet was curiously unaffected by her beauty. He had often wondered if she knew what a striking appearance she made, but he had never asked.

"I wish I could come with you," he said softly.

Jessie studied his face, her eyes searching his. "Can you?" He had never heard her sound so vulnerable.

Brad shifted position nervously, and she moved out of his arms. He ran his fingers through his white-blond hair as he spoke. "Jess, you know I can't. I only have a few days off, and I'm saving them . . . so we can spend Christmas together."

"Sure," she said flatly. The vulnerable moment had passed. "Brad, I'll have to see what happens when I get home. I may not be back for . . ."

"For the holidays?" he finished. "Jess, what about our plans?"

"Umhmmm, excuse me, Miss," the elderly ticket agent cleared his throat and interrupted the conversation with an embarrassed smile. "Here's your boarding pass. You only have a few minutes."

Brad glared at the ticket agent as Jessie thanked him and took her ticket. She turned to Brad quietly. "It's time for me to go."

"I love you, Jessie." Brad looked at her anxiously.

"I know." Before he could say more, Jessie turned and walked through the gate. Brad watched until she was out of sight. Muttering to himself, he hit the chair where Jessie had been sitting and strode out the glass doors of the terminal into the night.

* * *

As Jessie sank into her seat near the front of the plane she glanced at the passengers nearby. They were mostly weary-looking businessmen, engrossed in paperwork or sleeping with books in their laps. No one seemed even the slightest bit disposed to start a conversation, and Jessie was glad.

She fastened her seat belt and picked up the in-flight magazine in the seat pocket. Flipping through pages without really seeing them, she recalled Brad's expression as they parted. Why hadn't she been able to reciprocate when he said, "I love you"? Probably because he had expected her to. She shook her head almost imperceptibly as if to clear her thoughts of Brad. Why was she thinking of him at a time like this? It was all too confusing . . . such a nightmare. She smacked the magazine shut, reclined her seat, and closed her eyes.

Even after a kindly stewardess offered Jessie a pillow, sleep would not come. Instead, she found herself trying to sort out the events of the day. Could it have been only this afternoon that Gram called? It seemed a lifetime ago, yet etched into her memory for all time. In a deceptively ordinary moment, her life was changed forever. Was that the way all tragedy happened?

Jessie had been in the newsroom of the university paper where she worked, proofreading a feature article for the Sunday supplement. Having recently completed the university's graduate program in journalism, Jessie had agreed to stay on as managing editor through the end of the year. She loved her hours in the newsroom, selecting photos, reading wire-service copy, and encouraging first-year students. She often went there when she was homesick—the smell of newsprint evoked memories of the happy hours she'd spent playing under her father's old walnut desk at his newspaper in the small New England community that was her home.

Jessie had been leaning over the feature story, cup of coffee in hand, when Sarah, the copy chief, poked her head into Jessie's office.

"Phone, Jessie. It's long distance I think."

"Transfer it in here," Jessie answered, still reading.

"Hello?" she said absently a few moments later. "Gram?"

Jessie listened and set her cup down hard. The hot coffee sloshed onto her hand and onto the galley sheet, but she didn't wipe it up. Instead, she picked up a pencil and scrawled a flight number and a departure time on a scrap of paper. "I'm coming, Gram," she whispered and placed the receiver in its cradle.

Jessie opened her office door and stepped into the confusion and bustle of the newsroom. Sarah, who was on her way back to Jessie's office with an arm full of wire-service stories, dropped them on a nearby table when she saw her friend's face.

"Jessie, what's happened?" Sarah gently took her arm and guided her down a quiet hall.

"My parents have been killed. An auto accident." Jessie thought her own voice sounded hoarse, as if someone else was speaking. "They're dead."

"Both of them?" Sarah cried the words incredulously. She put her arm around Jessie's shoulders, and they began the long walk across the campus to Jessie's apartment.

*   *   *

"Excuse me, Miss," the voice jolted Jessie back to the present. "I wondered if you'd like anything . . . a soft drink or a cocktail?" The stewardess asked the question solicitously, bending low over Jessie's seat.

"Why, no . . . no thank you," Jessie murmured politely, a little confused at being drawn out of her reverie so abruptly. The stewardess seemed to be looking at Jessie's sweater. Jessie glanced down and blushed. It was soaked with tears. She awkwardly pulled a tissue out of her pocket and dabbed her eyes. As she did, she realized her cheeks were hot with moisture. How long had she been sitting here crying silently?

"I'll be fine, thanks," Jessie told the stewardess firmly.

The woman smiled brightly and squeezed Jessie's shoulder.

"I'll tell you one thing, honey," she whispered. "Whoever he is, he's not worth the trouble."

Jessie smiled stiffly and nodded. The stewardess moved her beverage cart down the aisle.

Reaching into her purse, Jessie quickly retrieved a compact, powdered her nose, and applied a little lipstick. With a firm resolve to stop crying, she closed her eyes once again.

This time her thoughts turned to pleasant things, memories of her childhood mostly. She could see Mother and Dad sitting in the white swing on the porch of their home, watching their only child romp in the newly fallen leaves.

"Daddy," the little girl called coyly, "Daddy, come find me!"

The tall, quiet man slowly lifted himself from his seat in the swing and looked over the yard in mock consternation.

"Mama, where is my dark-haired princess? I can't find her. Where can she be?"

Mama giggled and Daddy winked. With exaggerated concern, he walked across the yard in the golden autumn sun, looking first under the forsythia bushes and then behind the old car.

"Jessie, Jessie," he called.

Just when the little girl thought she couldn't wait one more minute, he rustled the pile of leaves by her head.

"Why, Mama, here she is!" he yelled in surprise. "Imagine that. A princess buried in the leaves."

With that, Daddy let out a whoop and jumped in the pile of leaves with Jessie. They rolled and laughed until there was no breath in either of them.

Jessie and her dad had played the game every November of her childhood. It was, in fact, just about that time of year again. With the realization, Jessie felt a stab of pain, mingled with a deep sense of joy, at the memory.

The plane arrived in Boston in the wee hours of the morning. Jessie deplaned quickly; she was anxious to get out

11

of the close quarters after the long flight. She had napped fitfully the last half of the trip, but she didn't feel rested. Behind her eyelids her eyes felt dry, and she blinked several times as she emerged into the glare of another airport. Who would be here to meet her? Surely, not Gram at this time of the morning.

She saw Uncle Charles immediately. His likeness to her father made her falter for an instant. Maybe this was all a dream.

"Jessie," he said earnestly as he embraced her. "Honey, welcome home. I'm so sorry."

I'm sorry, Jessie thought. Weren't those the same words Brad had used? And for what good reason—words didn't change anything. She found herself feeling strangely angry.

"Hi," she said in a stony voice. "I'm sorry too."

Uncle Charles looked at her quizzically but didn't comment.

"Let's find your luggage," he said. "We've got a long drive to your grandmother's. I imagine she'll have breakfast for you when we get there. You must be tired. I've taken enough of those 'red-eye' flights to know they can be exhausting."

Uncle Charles retrieved Jessie's luggage while she waited in his car parked on the airport circle. The sleepy city was beginning to stir, and the noises of the morning traffic signaled a metropolis coming to life. Jessie studied Uncle Charles' obviously new luxury car. Dad had never driven a car like this, she mused. But what a price Uncle Charles had paid for making it big in the newspaper business, sacrificing all family relationships for the sake of prosperity.

His voice interrupted her thoughts.

"Honey, hand me those keys and I'll put your suitcase in the back. You certainly travel light for a woman. But then, I guess someone as pretty as you doesn't have to do much sprucing up. No wonder your daddy always called you 'Princess' . . ." Uncle Charles' voice trailed off, and he stumbled over the last word.

Jessie felt a surge of compassion for this man, an uncle whom she hardly knew.

"It's OK," she said, squeezing his arm. "Here are your keys. Can I help?"

Uncle Charles smiled gratefully, and Jessie realized that, for whatever reasons, the death of her parents was a tragedy for him too. He loaded the luggage in a hurry, and they set off down the interstate.

For a long time they drove in silence, neither one trying to make small talk as Uncle Charles maneuvered through the maze of traffic. As they passed the outskirts of the city, Jessie turned to her uncle.

"How did it happen?" She said the words matter-of-factly, knowing they needed no explanation.

Uncle Charles spoke haltingly. "I don't know all the details myself. Mom called me early this morning—yesterday morning I guess it is now—it seems your folks were headed out of town for a few days vacation. They crossed the center line and were struck head-on by a truck . . . a delivery truck of some sort."

Jessie didn't answer. After a while, they talked about other things—the unseasonably warm morning, distant relatives, Jessie's work in California. Soon Charles pulled to a stop in front of Jessie's childhood home—the home Gram shared with Jessie and her parents. Her eyes searched the large white house in vain for a sign of familiar movement. Dad's car was not in the gravel driveway, but Mother's flower bed was freshly tended, a deep mulch of russet maple leaves covering the sleeping bulbs for the coming winter. On the porch lay Hurst, the Irish setter. He raised his head and thumped his tail twice on the wooden planks as he casually regarded the intruders.

Uncle Charles was at Jessie's car door, opening it for her before she realized it.

"Here, honey, watch your step."

Jessie didn't like being made a fuss over. She waved Uncle Charles' hand away and walked briskly to the house, stopping briefly to scratch Hurst behind the ears.

"Hello, boy. Have you missed me?" Hurst ran an excited circle around Jessie and followed her inside the front door.

"Gram," she called loudly. "Gram. It's Jessie. Where are you?"

"I'm here, Jessica." Gram's words preceded her down the long hallway to the kitchen.

They met each other halfway as Uncle Charles stood back and watched the reunion. The older Jessica Sterling was tall, like her namesake, and thin. She had aged gracefully and with dignity. She stood erect and her silver hair haloed her face softly. By all appearances, the two women embracing could have been the same one, born in different eras.

Arms around one another's waists, Jessie and Gram made their way down the hall. Jessie had both hands wrapped around a cup of steaming hot tea when Charles entered the kitchen.

"Your bag is up in your room," he said a little too cheerfully. "I've got to be at work in 45 minutes."

Gram nodded and offered to prepare him a thermos of coffee and some homemade muffins to go.

He's a workaholic, Jessie thought disdainfully. No wonder he never married. No wonder he never came around to see us.

While Charles waited for Gram to pack his breakfast, he turned to Jessie.

"I want to help you all I can, Jessie." He paused as if he wanted to say more. Jessie wasn't ready to hear it—not from him, not yet.

Gram, who always seemed to sense Jessie's moods, came to her rescue.

"Thank you, son," she answered firmly. "We'll be fine for now."

She took his arm and they walked quietly to the front door. Jessie could hear Gram murmuring in a low voice to Charles, something about "the business," something about "it's too soon."

Jessie picked up the spoon from Gram's silver service, which was resting near the sugar bowl on the old oak table. Absently, she dropped a lump of sugar in her china cup and began to stir. She stirred the tea slowly, gazing at it without

14

seeing. The heavy front door closed with a muffled thud. The sound of a car engine filtered through the air. When Gram re-entered the sunny kitchen, Jessie sat soberly at the table, still stirring her tea.

2
·····

A FINE MIST HUNG IN THE AIR as Jessie stepped from the limousine. Shivering, she breathed deeply. The close, perfumed air in the chapel had made her feel as though she were drowning as the room filled with mourners. Now, at the graveside, she lifted her head and watched as faces from her childhood gathered under the canopy.

The funeral director had placed chairs for her and Gram near the head of the caskets. Holding Gram's arm, Jessie lowered her into one of the chairs. How composed the older lady seemed. Jessie had always assumed she would bury her parents someday. Not at the same time, perhaps, and not yet—not so soon. But Gram could never have foreseen outliving her son and daughter-in-law. What was holding her together?

Jessie swallowed a sob, and rather than taking the seat next to Gram, stepped behind Gram's chair and stood, one hand on each of her grandmother's shoulders. The tension gripping her body was all that held her together. If she relaxed, took a seat, let her guard down for even a moment, grief would overtake her. She mustn't give in.

A brisk wind sliced through the gathering. Jessie pulled the collar of her mother's cashmere coat close around her face. In shock and disbelief after Gram's call, she hadn't given a thought to the cold New England weather she would be exposed to in early November. Now, wrapped in her mother's garment, the hemline and the sleeves just a shade too short, she inhaled the slightest hint of her mother's favorite fragrance. In that instant, Jessie's wall of self-reliance trembled beneath the weight of her sorrow. She felt her knees go weak

16

and the sea of familiar faces began to spin. Suddenly, some-one's arm was behind her back, holding her up.

"Here, let me help you to your seat."

"No, I can't sit down," Jessie mumbled. "Please, I'm all right now. I'll be fine." She didn't turn her head in the direction of the male voice. She had no desire to see whose arm was supporting her. She only wanted this to be over.

As the pastor's compassionate voice concluded the final prayer, her grandmother rose to her feet, and Jessie moved to stand next to her. Many of Gram's friends from church filed past and offered their condolences. Old friends of her parents took Jessie's hand or patted her arm, shaking their heads in dismay. Jessie responded unthinkingly to each murmured expression of sympathy. She stared blankly into the concerned eyes of the kindly people and, biting her bottom lip, made all the correct responses.

As the pastor of Gram's church stepped up to her, he took both her hands and held them tightly against his chest.

"Jessie, my dear, I had come to know your parents well during the last few months. They attended services quite regularly. Fine people . . . fine people. And so proud of you. Scared you would settle in California though, and they wouldn't be able to see much of you . . . er, a . . . well . . . your grandmother is getting up in years. It's good the two of you will have each other to see you through . . . with God's help. We'll be praying for you and your grandmother, Jessie. Lean on the Lord, child. You'll get through this with His help."

The Lord? Dad had told her in one of their weekly telephone conversations that he and Mom had been attending church. How could God have let them down like this?

The pastor was right about one thing, Jessie thought. She *would* get through this. For Gram's sake, she looked in the Reverend's eyes and replied woodenly, "Thank you, you're very kind."

Gram and Uncle Charles had moved apart from the other mourners and stood together, Charles' arm draped protectively around Gram's shoulders. Jessie could see they were in deep conversation, so she stood aside. Studying Uncle

Charles, she was, as always, taken aback by how like Dad he was. The same eyes surrounded by the same tiny lines that, no matter how serious the conversation, belied the fact that he was a man who loved to laugh. Of course, Uncle Charles wasn't laughing now. He looked genuinely grieved. Jessie wondered if on this day he regretted his treatment of his twin. Perhaps his grief wasn't only the loss of his brother— perhaps he was hurting for Gram. Perhaps he was feeling guilty that his relationship with Philip had faltered over the years. Jessie knew that Dad and Uncle Charles had been inseparable as children and young men. They had played on the same high school football team and had attended the same college. And when they were ready to face the adult world, Grandpa had welcomed them both into his newspaper —giving them responsibilities that would groom them for running the paper someday.

It had worked out well for Uncle Charles. But Jessie's dad found himself out in the cold when Charles became greedy and decided he didn't want to share the newspaper with his twin. Philip graciously left the business without causing a flap. He started his own little paper—not much competition for Uncle Charles' large daily, but it provided well for his small family. Dad had often said it would be Jessie's job to develop the paper into as large an operation as Uncle Charles enjoyed. He just didn't seem to have the heart to make it big.

Jessie had overheard many conversations between he and her mom. Mom encouraged him to take the risks and pay the price to garner a fair share of the subscription market, but Dad was full of reasons not to. He was happy, he said, with the paper just the way it was. He was comfortable with his better-safe-than-sorry style of reporting. Mom never complained, and certainly never voiced her dissatisfaction to Jessie, but Jessie could tell, nonetheless, that her mother thought Dad was capable of chewing a lot more than he was willing to bite off. Jessie had always been of the silent opinion that when Uncle Charles had squeezed Dad out of the family business, it had cost Dad more than his share of big profits. It had cost him his spirit and his drive and his confidence.

Maybe Dad had forgiven his brother for that—but Jessie didn't feel Uncle Charles deserved forgiveness. Jessie made a mental note to ask Gram about the details of their parting of the ways. Now that Mom and Dad were gone, Gram might be more willing to discuss it. All that Jessie really knew was what she had pieced together from snatches of conversation over the years.

Jessie watched as Gram and Uncle Charles embraced and turned to walk toward her. Uncle Charles' eyes met Jessie's and he spoke, his voice full of emotion.

"Jessie, honey, if there's anything I can do for you, please let me know. In a few days, when you're feeling stronger, you'll need to get down to your dad's paper. It's yours now, Jessie. The folks that worked for your dad are going to be anxious about their futures. They're going to want to meet with you—most of them remember you as a schoolgirl, not a business owner and certainly not as their boss.

"But, this isn't a good time to talk business. Your dad always told me I don't think about anything else. I guess this proves that he was right and that I have very questionable taste. Forgive me, honey. I'll be by the house in a few days to see if I can help you. You and your gram take care of each other, now."

Jessie nodded mutely and turned and locked her arm through Gram's, and they walked toward the limousine. The driver held the door open for them. As she was about to step in, Jessie looked back toward the identical caskets. The gravesite was practically deserted now, but clusters of mourners stood together near their cars, despairing over the loss of their friends and the enormity of Jessie's and Gram's sorrow.

As Jessie looked on, two men in workclothes moved toward the caskets and began to lower them into the cold, soggy ground. Gram touched her arm. "Let's go now, honey."

Jessie allowed Gram to lead her into the limo, never taking her eyes from the strange men and their grisly task. As the driver took his place behind the wheel and slowly pulled away, Jessie lowered her head, covering her face with her hands.

3
·····

*F*OR THE NEXT TWO DAYS the house was full of friends and family, all wanting to help Gram and Jessie with the healing process, all feeling painfully inadequate. Gram reacted typically for a woman of her high energy level. She stayed constantly busy. As the well-meaning visitors brought in food, Gram met them at the door and ushered them into her kitchen, where she occupied her guests with constant conversation. Rarely did she break down. As she talked of her lost loved ones, her eyes often filled with tears, but she kept her composure.

Jessie marveled at Gram's self-control. She knew that Gram counted her daughter-in-law's death as great a loss as that of her son. Philip and Lynn had lived with Gram since Grandpa's death, very early in their marriage.

Jessie's pain was more evident. Her mind and spirit were mercifully numbed. She found it difficult to concentrate on what was being said, her thoughts drifting as she and Hurst wandered aimlessly from room to room in the large, comfortable home that would never be the same. Every room reached out to embrace her with familiar scents and memories—precious, but too painful to allow her to linger. Usually talkative and outgoing, Jessie now wanted more than anything to be alone in this house . . . to absorb it . . . to remember . . . to forget.

In her parents' bedroom, Jessie sat on the end of the bed looking at herself in the mirror over the dresser. So this is the face of grief, she thought as she ran her fingers from her forehead down the curve of her cheek resting them on her chin as she studied herself. What will you do now, Jessie? Who will tell you that you're smart? Who will tell you that you're pretty? Who will walk you down the aisle? Who will spoil your children? Her future sprawled ahead of her as flat and unexciting as a midwinter Nebraska freeway.

Jessie stood and moved to her mother's large walk-in closet, opening the double doors wide. She moved her head slightly as she surveyed it all, taking in the neatness, the femininity, the essence that was her mother. She stepped in, touching each dress as she walked to the back where her mother's shoes rested in pairs on built-in shelves. Three worn shoe boxes were stacked on the bottom, and Jessie curiously lifted them to the top shelf and removed the lid of the first box.

Inside were snapshots of family and friends. Jessie thumbed through them listlessly. She didn't feel up to looking at them and dealing with the emotions they would evoke.

The second box contained papers her mother had felt necessary to keep on hand . . . her marriage certificate, Jessie's birth certificate, copies of insurance policies.

Jessie disinterestedly pulled the lid off the third box and found personal letters her mother had received over the years, separated into stacks according to writer and tied into neat little bundles. One bundle was from Mom's sister in Ohio, one stack written by Jessie's Grandmother Stevens before her death. The third bundle, containing only a few letters, all bore the return address of this house.

These must be letters that Dad wrote to Mom, Jessie mused. She opened the top letter and began to read.

Dear Lynn,

It was so wonderful seeing you recently when I was in Boston. Thank you for showing me the sights of that beautiful city. Even though I have been there many times, seeing the city with you was like seeing it for the first time.

It is my sincere hope that we will have some time to spend together next month when I come for a fraternity brother's wedding.

Until then, know that I am thinking of you often.

Love,
Charles

"Charles!" Jessie uttered the name hoarsely. What could this mean? She stared at his signature. Then, frowning her surprise, Jessie looked quickly at the envelope. It was post-dated in September, the year before her parents' marriage. Clutching the bundle of letters to her, Jessie sighed with relief.

But still, why would Charles be writing love letters to her mother? Well, maybe not a real love letter, but certainly there was more feeling involved than would be acceptable for a brother toward his twin's future wife. Jessie tried to think. How long did Mom and Dad know each other before they were married? She couldn't recall ever being told much about their courtship.

Urgently, she opened the next letters.

I see your face in my dreams . . . When I think of your laugh, it makes me smile . . . When will I be able to see you again? . . .

No, this was not standard sister-in-law-to-be correspondence. Jessie felt hot anger against Uncle Charles begin to burn. Had Dad known? Had Mom felt the same toward Uncle Charles as he felt toward her?

She opened the last envelope . . .

Dearest Lynn,

I received your letter two days ago, but I couldn't bring myself to answer right away. How I had hoped you would reconsider your words to me when we were last together. You are right, Lynn, you never encouraged me. And I certainly never intended to fall in love with you. But it happened, and I don't think I will ever be sorry.

You mentioned that you hoped we would not be uncomfortable with each other in the future. I assure you that my love for you is far too great to turn into anger or resentment because you have chosen another. Even if that other man is my own brother. I love him, too, Lynn. And I would never want to hurt him.

If you decide to tell him of the time we spent together, I will not deny it. I will, however, be most happy to tell him that I consider him to be the luckiest of men to have won the heart of the most beautiful and gracious lady I have ever known.

I will never regret loving you. . . .

Charles

Jessie dropped to the floor and sat cross-legged, staring at the handful of letters. She was torn between feeling she knew too much already and being determined to know more. Did Charles ever get over Mother? Did Mom ever tell Dad? Does Gram know? Would she dare bring it up with Charles? Did it even matter now?

Jessie put the letters back in the shoe box and put all three shoe boxes back on the bottom shelf. Curiously, she welcomed the diversion of this new information. It gave her something to consider besides her great loss and her overwhelming loneliness.

She walked across the bedroom her parents had shared and stood at the door, taking it all in. Somehow, she had never given much thought to Philip and Lynn Sterling having a life apart from their marriage to each other and their roles as parents. What a curious thing to consider, the young and lovely Lynn Stevens being pursued by brothers Charles and Philip Sterling.

She stepped into the large second floor hall and headed for the staircase down to Gram and the lingering guests. Wanting more than anything to retreat to her room, Jessie knew that Gram would appreciate her presence. And she also knew that soon enough this house would be all too empty.

She walked through the living room, nodding stiffly to

the faces that had arrived while she had been upstairs. In the kitchen, Gram sat at the large round oak table with several men and women. Jessie pulled up a chair and sat down. They heard the doorbell and Jessie started to get up and answer it.

Gram touched her arm, "Someone will get it, honey. Why don't you have something to eat? Please try."

Before Jessie could nod in acceptance, Delores Rogers set a plate in front of her. Cold roast beef sandwich and chips.

"Can I get you something to drink, sweetie?" Delores asked, forcing cheerfulness.

"Just a glass of milk would be fine, Mrs. Rogers." Jessie answered, picking up the sandwich, which actually looked quite appetizing. Just as she put it to her mouth, Uncle Charles walked into the kitchen.

"Hi, Mom, Jess," he gestured toward the front of the house. "Looks like you have plenty of folks keeping you company. How are you?"

"We're getting along, son," Gram answered.

Jessie stared silently. Had Mom ever regretted her choice? Charles was certainly the more successful of the Sterling twins. Had Mom and Charles ever spoken again of their time together? Had Uncle Charles' resentment of losing Mom prompted him to squeeze Dad out of the business? Jessie inhaled sharply at this new thought, causing Charles to turn his attention to her.

"How about you, honey? Are you OK?"

"I'm fine. What brings you here today?" What a rude question, Jessie reprimanded herself. He has every right to be here.

Uncle Charles' brow creased.

I've hurt his feelings, Jessie thought. "I just mean, I guess I wasn't expecting you till later in the week."

Charles smiled—he'd misunderstood.

"Actually, I needed to talk to you and Gram, Jessie." He looked first at Jessie and then to Gram. "I got a call from Dr. McCord this morning. As Phil and Lynn's doctor, he got a copy of the autopsy reports and death certificates in the mail today."

"This is a personal matter," Delores began ushering friends and neighbors out of the kitchen. "We'll just leave you alone together for a bit."

Gram and Jessie looked at Charles expectantly, knowing something unusual was contained in those reports for him to make a special trip to tell it.

"Lynn died instantly—a direct trauma to her head sustained at impact. But Phil . . . Phil suffered a massive heart attack behind the wheel that caused him to veer into the path of the truck. He would have died if he'd been sitting in his easy chair. But Lynn wouldn't have died with him."

Jessie stood up abruptly and left the room, her pace increasing as she walked through the living room, running as she ascended the stairs. Crying, she ran into her room and slammed the door.

"It's too much," she cried aloud. "I don't want to hear anymore." She flung herself facedown on the bed, sobbing.

Jessie wept unreservedly for the first time since she learned of the death of her parents. After many minutes, she lay exhausted, still facedown. She turned over onto her back, tears subsiding.

She knew Dad's doctor had been treating him for stress. She knew that he worried constantly about keeping his business afloat. Finally, the years of struggling had conquered him, and in the process, had killed her mother.

Struggle . . . years of struggle . . . created by the unmitigated greed and jealousy of one Charles Eugene Sterling. Suddenly, it all seemed very clear. If it hadn't been for Charles, none of this would have happened.

"I don't know how," Jessie determined in her heart, "and I don't know when. But I'll make him pay for this."

Jessie could taste the hatred . . . and she savored the flavor of it.

4
•••••

*J*ESSIE AWOKE AND STRETCHED SI-
LENTLY, the familiarity of her childhood room wrapping
around her and giving her comfort. She had slept well for the
first time since Gram's call. Last night, at Gram's insistence,
she had taken a mild sedative prescribed by Gram's doctor.
He had been at the funeral, Gram had announced, as she persuaded Jessie to take his medication. As if, somehow, that
would legitimize the fact that for the first time in her life
Jessie was ingesting a substance she considered a crutch for
the weak-kneed. But, this morning she had to admit that she
felt clearheaded and rested. For the first time in what seemed
like a long time, she felt the stirrings of her old self.

She looked around her room and recalled the Jessica
Sterling who had grown up in these surroundings. Strong-
minded and sure of herself, Jessie had lived her life as the
only child of parents who thought she was the most wonderful child ever born. She had never known real unhappiness—
just the usual broken teenage romances, or an occasional
grounding for talking back to her mother. Her life had been
one of security, love, and hope. The foundations of her security had been badly shaken by her parents' death, but the
love and hope were still as much a part of her as her flawless
skin and green eyes.

Always given to laughter, Jessie drew people to her easily.
Having been accepted and cherished herself, she reached out
to others with an honesty and openness that made them feel
valuable. Jessie genuinely liked people, and they liked her.
Only lately, since the accident, she found herself wanting to

26

blame someone. And Uncle Charles was that someone. Silently, bitterness was growing in her heart. Not quite sure of his role in her parents' accident, she believed he was indirectly responsible, if only because he had robbed her father of the happiness he deserved.

Jessie swept her thick black hair back from her face as she rose. Putting Charles out of her mind, she decided on a quick shower and a brisk walk through the neighborhood before breakfast. She thought she could hear Gram downstairs already. It was impossible to beat that woman out of bed in the morning!

After showering, Jessie wrapped herself in a thick white terrycloth robe and stepped to the vanity. She fastened her hair into a simple ponytail and brushed her teeth. Just a little color on her cheeks and lips would do for now. Jessie rarely wore much makeup—she couldn't see enough difference in her appearance to merit the time. Her green eyes were framed by black lashes and eyebrows, and she usually was browned by the sun and needed nothing to enhance her aquiline bone structure and good skin. But, since leaving California, the tan was beginning to fade, so she quickly brushed a little color onto her cheeks.

Jessie pulled on her sweats and sat on the edge of the bed to put on her socks and tennis shoes. As she smoothed the bedding and pulled the bedspread into place, she thought she heard the doorbell. Gram will get it, she decided, as she plumped up the pillows and gave the bed a final pat. She left her sunny room and went into the hall and down the stairs as she heard Gram open the front door and welcome someone in.

As she entered the living room, Gram was talking to a tall, youngish looking man—certainly no one that would be a contemporary of her parents or of Gram. He turned and watched her walk across the large room toward them. His eyes widened and his head tilted quizzically at her vibrancy and energy. This was a very beautiful young woman. When he had stepped up behind her and put his arm around her to steady her at the cemetery, he would never have guessed that she would have such a striking presence or that she would make such a large room seem so completely full.

Jessie's sneaker-clad feet made scarcely a sound on the gleaming hardwood floor as she moved in long-legged, graceful strides toward the handsome young man and her grandmother.

"Jessie, darling, I want you to meet my friend, Spencer McCord. Spencer, this is my granddaughter, Jessica Sterling."

"How do you do," they spoke simultaneously, each stretching forward their right hand. As his heavily-browed hazel eyes met hers over their clasped hands, Jessie's self-assurance faltered noticeably. She looked down fleetingly and then back up into his unwavering eyes, smiling foolishly and withdrawing her hand, knowing full well that she had stumbled over her composure and desperately hoping he hadn't perceived her to be the empty-headed, helpless female-type she deplored.

If Gram noticed Jessie's sudden muteness, she didn't let on. "Jessie, Spence is the doctor who sent over the sedative I gave you last night. Tell us, how did you sleep?"

"Well, very well," Jessie looked at Gram gratefully. Her composure was returning, and she was thankful to Gram for saying something—anything.

She turned back to Spence, feeling a need to explain her stance on sleeping medication. "It's the first time in my life I've taken anything like that, but Gram insisted. I don't plan on doing it again, but it was nice to get a good night's rest."

"Well, this is a difficult time for you. I certainly wouldn't recommend a sleeping aid long-term for any of my patients. You look like you're dressed for some exercise. Am I right?"

"Yes, I run, but today I had planned to walk. It's been a while," Jessie answered.

"Excuse me," Gram interrupted. "The coffee should be ready. I'll be right back with it."

"Well, once you're back to your usual activities—particularly exercise—I'm sure your sleeping difficulties will disappear."

"Did Gram ask you to come here this morning because

she's worried about me?" Jessie asked pointedly. "I'm sure you don't make house calls as a rule, do you?"

"No, I don't," Spence laughed. "Your grandmother and my mother are great friends, and, of course, I know your grandmother from our church, and now she's my patient. But she was my friend first, and very kind and attentive to my mother when we lost my dad. I wanted to check on her. Actually, I've known you, too, Jessie . . . when you were a child. When I was a teenager, you were a ponytailed little girl coming to Sunday School with your grandma. I didn't have a clue you would grow up to be so beautiful, or I would have done something outrageous to get your attention."

Jessie was surprised at his directness. She didn't know whether to say thank you or ignore the compliment. She stared at him blankly, vaguely aware that her face was getting hot and probably pink, and acutely aware that her heart was beginning to pound so wildly in her chest that she was afraid he could hear it.

Again, Gram saved her from embarrassment by noisily reentering the room carrying a plastic tray bearing the Mr. Coffee coffeepot, a half-pint container of half-and-half, a handful of sugar cubes, and three everyday, well-used coffee mugs.

"I hope I didn't keep you waiting," Gram announced nervously.

How unlike Gram to serve a guest like this, Jessie thought. She always jumps at the chance to get out the silver service and make a friend's visit a real occasion. Suddenly Jessie realized this was for her sake. Gram had noticed her uneasiness and had settled on this old plastic tray to save Jessie from being alone with this man who obviously had robbed her of her adult composure with a handshake and simple hello.

Spence had been to this home many times before, and he, too, knew Gram was breaking a years-long tradition of gracious entertaining. He looked over at Jessie, and she returned his gaze. They both realized at the same moment that their instantaneous mutual attraction was not only obvious to each other but to Gram as well. Suddenly, they both smiled broadly, and then, glancing at Gram's puzzled look, began to laugh out loud. Jessie laughed with the delight of realizing her life would go on, Spence laughed with joy at discovering this winsome young woman, and Gram began to laugh because— well, because they were.

5

•••••

JESSIE STEPPED FROM THE SHOWER and reached for her robe. Taking a large bathtowel, she wrapped it deftly, turban-style, around her wet hair. Already laid out on her bed were her favorite sweater and skirt. The khaki sweater did great things for her green eyes, and she knew it. The matching skirt was a black and khaki print. She would wear her black suede boots with the medium heel.

Dinner with Spencer McCord. Anticipation of this magnitude had evaded her since high school. She had known, of course, from their first conversation that they would see each other again. Love at first sight is definitely out of vogue, she told herself, smiling. And she was certainly beyond trying to build a relationship out of good bone structure and an athletic build. Still, there was a quiet strength in this young doctor—a directness and self-assurance—that was so appealing. Had she met her match? She hoped so. Or, maybe she hoped not. She wasn't quite sure. But she certainly wanted to look her best for their evening together.

As she towel-dried her dark hair and combed through it, she thought back to a special occasion a few years ago when her mother had spent a great deal of time primping in front of the mirror. As Mom had walked into the den where Jessie and her dad sat waiting, Jessie had exclaimed, "Oh, Mother, you look sensational!"

"Yes, Jessie," her father had interjected, "your beautiful mother looks exactly the same today as she did the day I mar-

31

ried her. It just takes her more time in front of the mirror to look that way now."

Mom had pretended indignation, and Dad had laughed uproariously at himself. Mom had told him he was his own best audience. How they enjoyed each other. How Jessie had loved them. When would she be able to think about her life with them without this stab of pain, wounding her already sore heart?

Jessie dressed carefully for this important evening. No denying it, she wanted to impress him. She wondered where they would go for dinner, what they would talk about—would he compliment her appearance as he had the morning they met? Was he experiencing the same anticipation as he showered and dressed at his apartment?

The shrill ringing of the telephone startled Jessie back to reality.

"Jessie," Gram's voice floated up the stairs. "Phone's for you."

She walked to the phone on her bedside table and picked up the receiver. Her hand flew to her mouth in a guilty gesture as she recognized Brad's voice.

"Brad, how are you?"

"Not so good, Jess. I'm missing my girl. I just thought I'd call and see if you'd be back in time for Thanksgiving."

"Oh, Brad. I should have called. I've been so busy trying to get Mom's and Dad's affairs in order . . . I don't expect to be back for several weeks yet. I own Dad's paper now, Brad. There's a lot to be settled before I leave."

Brad's sigh was audible. "I'm afraid you'll never come back, Jess. Do you think that's what's going to happen?"

"Brad, please. I can't think past tomorrow right now. I just have to take my life one day at a time."

"OK, Jess." Brad's voice had a self-pitying quality Jessie recognized clearly. "Do what you need to do and don't worry about me. You know where to find me if you need me."

As usual, Brad was saying all the right words. And, as usual, they were stirring up all the wrong feelings. Instead of feeling reassured, Jessie felt guilty and conniving. Why didn't she tell him that in addition to all the business she must attend to, there was someone here who made her feel like a schoolgirl, not a mother figure?

Brad's call had a slight dampening effect on Jessie's mood. But after saying good-bye and turning her thoughts back to Spence, it didn't take long for the anticipation to return.

By the time she had put on the finishing touches and was taking one final look at herself in the full-length mirror on the back of her bedroom door, she heard Gram's voice welcoming Spence. Grabbing her small handbag from the dresser, Jessie hurried down the stairs to greet him. As he turned to her, his face lit up noticeably.

"You look great. It's good to see you."

"I've been looking forward to seeing you, too, Spence." Jessie was surprised at her own honesty.

"I hope you don't mind stopping by my place, Jessie. I was tied up at the hospital and I haven't had a chance to clean up. It won't take me more than 15 minutes to shower and shave. Do you mind?"

Jessie smiled agreeably, "I don't mind at all."

Obviously he hadn't spent an hour and a half getting ready and looking forward to their meeting. Somehow, though, it didn't matter to her. It was clear he was happy to be with her now, and she would get all of his attention for the remainder of the evening.

After a quick farewell to Gram, they stepped out into the cold November night. Once inside the car, Spencer talked of his day at the hospital and of patients he was particularly concerned about. Jessie watched his profile as he drove and was moved by his sincerity as he asked her how she and Gram were handling their grief. She was able to tell him honestly that, though a thread of pain still ran through her heart, she was beginning to think of her parents with joy and with gratitude for the start in life they had given her.

Inside Spence's apartment, while she waited for him to shower and shave, Jessie surveyed his living room. One wall was floor to ceiling bookshelves—completely full. Though the books were stacked neatly, their varying heights and widths gave the shelves a look of disarray. A small television sat in the corner, not positioned to be seen from any seat in the room. The sofa pillows had a showroom appearance, giving Jessie the impression the sofa was seldom used.

Sitting a couple of feet out in front of the wall of bookshelves was Spence's chair. This was obviously where he spent his leisure time. A floor lamp with a worn, cockeyed shade stood just slightly behind and to the left of the sagging chair. In neat stacks on the floor were books—medical-looking journals, mostly—newspapers and a few issues of *Newsweek*.

On the left arm of the chair was Spence's Bible. As Jessie lowered herself into his chair, she picked up the worn, leather Bible and began to thumb through it. On almost every page there were underlined scriptures. *Blessed is the man that walketh not in the counsel of the ungodly . . . Thou wilt keep him in perfect peace, whose mind is stayed on thee . . . If any of you lack wisdom, let him ask of God, that giveth to all men liberally . . .*

For a reason she couldn't explain, Jessie felt as though she were looking through his personal mail. Yet she didn't put the Bible down. She ran her fingers down the worn pages, stopping at each marked passage, wondering how these words applied to the life of a vital, handsome, successful young doctor.

She thought fleetingly of her own Bible, given to her by Gram years ago when Jessie had gone forward at Gram's church and made a profession of faith. Where, she wondered, could that Bible be now? She suspected she hadn't had it in her hands since she left home for college—and likely it had not been read with regularity before that. Looking at Spence's Bible now, Jessie wished she had more in common with the child she had been when she walked down the aisle at Gram's church.

She hurriedly replaced Spence's Bible on the arm of his chair and stood as he entered the room.

"That was fast," she smiled at him. "This is an interesting room—I believe it's called organized clutter."

"Well, I don't spend a lot of time here. Some nights I just

stay in the doctors' quarters at the hospital. When I do have an evening to spend at home, I have a lot of reading I like to catch up on—and no time to fuss with the decor." Spence was not the least embarrassed by his modest apartment. It met his needs.

Jessie thought of Brad, so anxious to live the good life on the income he would command when his residency was completed. Brad had big dreams, and Jessie knew he wanted her to be part of those dreams. Somehow those plans seemed excessive when compared to this quiet man who lived in this small apartment and spent many nights at the hospital to be near the patients who trusted him.

Brad—it had been two weeks since she had left California. She hadn't really even given him much thought until his call earlier this evening. Jessie pushed him from her mind now. She was going to have to deal with her feelings for Brad. She knew those feelings weren't strong enough to warrant marriage. And she knew that marriage was what Brad wanted from her.

Spence was holding her coat.

"Hungry?" His hand rested just a moment on her shoulders as he slipped it on.

"Starving."

"Just a minute, I forgot my pager." Spence hurried back to his bedroom and returned in seconds. "Let's go."

Jessie smiled to herself. Spence was certainly different from Brad, who left his pager at home deliberately so they wouldn't be disturbed. Jessie had always been flattered by Brad's attentiveness.

She glanced into Spence's eyes as he held the door open for her. By the time he pulled it closed behind them and took her arm, thoughts of Brad were as far away as the California beaches they once strolled together.

* * *

Seated at the restaurant, Spence and Jessie chatted easily. She spoke freely of her parents and her childhood. She told him about her job—her indefinite leave of absence . . . her

35

friend and coworker, Sarah. She even mentioned that there was someone that she had been dating for some time, but that they hadn't made a commitment.

Spence listened quietly. She was more talkative than he, but they both felt comfortable and at ease with one another. He shared more with her about his work, his commitment to his practice and the demanding nature of it on his time.

They were waiting for the dessert to be served, when Spence waved and smiled over her shoulder at someone coming into the restaurant.

"Well, good evening, Spence. Good to see you. And how is this pretty thing sitting here with you?"

Without turning her head, Jessie recognized the voice, so like her dad's. Charles.

Stiffly, she raised her eyes. Frozen, her lips would not smile.

She stared into his face mutely.

"Jessie, are you all right?"

"Yes, I'm fine." Her voice, thin and strained, pushed its way through her constricted throat. "Please excuse me, I'm going to find the powder room."

Spence stood as she left the table, and he and Charles, both puzzled and embarrassed, watched as she hurried away.

Safely out of their sight in the ladies' room, Jessie leaned against the door. She wasn't ready to face Charles. She hadn't expected to run into him like this. Jessie stood upright, relinquishing the support of the door.

OK, now. Pulling herself to her full height, and taking a deep breath, she reasoned with herself. Don't let this spoil the evening. Surely, I can be civil to Charles for a few moments.

One quick look in the mirror, and Jessie set her jaw in determination. Returning to the table, she was surprised to see that Charles was no longer there. She'd been gone only a few minutes.

Spence stood once again as she approached the table, and he held her chair.

"Where's Charles?" Jessie said, hoping she sounded nonchalant.

"He left. Jessie, what happened? Are you ill? Should we leave?"

"Oh, no, really. I'm fine. I was so surprised to see Charles." Jessie picked up her crumpled napkin and nervously began smoothing it on the table.

"There's more to it than that. You looked as if you'd seen a ghost. Is it his resemblance to your father? He and I decided that must be it. That's why he left. He said he'd come by your house soon and try to help you work through it."

"Oh, Spence. It's more than that. But I don't want to spoil our evening by thinking about Charles."

"What has happened, Jess? Charles is a friend of mine. I'm sure he would never want to upset you. If he's done something, it was unintentional."

"Oh, I'm sure it was unintentional." Jessie's eyes clouded and color rose in her cheeks. "I'm sure he only meant to make my father's life miserable—actually killing my parents was, of course, unintentional!"

"Jessie," Spence covered her trembling hand with his. "What's this about? Your dad had a heart attack and lost control of his car—that was no one's fault."

"Charles told me himself that you had been treating Dad for stress-related problems, Spence. Did you know that Charles was the main source of Dad's problems? Everyone knows that Charles and Dad couldn't run the paper together . . . and my dad was the one that lost out. While Charles was sitting back and getting rich off Grandpa's business, my dad was killing himself, trying to start a new paper."

Frowning, Spence watched Jessie intently as she continued.

"And Charles was in love with my mother years ago. Before she married Dad. Did you know that? I found some letters he had written her. He never married, rarely came around the family. He never got over it—he just got even. Oh, I know he didn't set out to kill them. But he set out to make them miserable, and he killed them in the process—unintentionally, as you say."

"Jessie, don't do this to yourself. I don't know about

37

Charles and your mother. But I know Charles. He's a good man."

Jessie looked into his eyes, puzzled.

"Spence, I know you mean well. But I don't think you can possibly understand what I'm feeling."

"I know what hate can do. It will hurt you more than it will ever hurt Charles. Don't give in to it, Jessie."

"I don't know if I can help it. I miss them so much."

"Promise me you'll try." Tenderly, he reached up and brushed away a tear. His hand rested on her cheek.

"Don't ruin your own life over this, Jessie." He had leaned so close she could feel his breath against her face. His intensity almost frightened her, but she didn't move away.

Suddenly, the pager he wore broke the silence. Spence relaxed back into his chair and reached down to shut it off.

"Will you excuse me a moment? I need to call the hospital."

Before Jessie could respond, he was out of his seat.

* * *

Jessie watched as Spence's back disappeared from view. The evening hadn't gone exactly as she had hoped, but it wasn't a total loss, either. Except for the interruption by Charles, it had been very enjoyable.

Charles . . . how she wished she knew the whole story of Charles. Although she had never known him well, she had never considered him a mysterious sort. Just a close relative that remained at arm's length. It wasn't that she had always hated him—although she knew he had caused Dad unhappiness—she really had never even given him much thought until now.

But now, she recoiled at the thought of him. His life had been intertwined with the lives of her parents in a way she had been unaware of. Somehow that made him seem mysterious and a little on the "shady" side. Subconsciously, Charles' aloofness during her childhood coupled with the fact that he had been successful in business—Grandpa's business—while Dad had to go it alone in a smaller, less successful venture were all Jessie needed to indict him. The un-revealed relationship with her mother added to the hostility Jessie felt. The final blow was seeing him here tonight, smiling and chatting, his face, voice, and actions a mirror of the father that was lost to her forever.

Engrossed in her thoughts, Jessie was startled when Spence suddenly appeared at her side.

"Jessie, I'm sorry to have to cut this short, but I'm needed at the hospital. I may be tied up for hours. I've called you a cab. It will be here any minute."

As they moved to the front of the restaurant where their coats had been checked, Spence held Jessie's arm.

"My mother is calling your grandmother tonight to invite the two of you to spend Thanksgiving with us. I hope you'll accept."

"That sounds wonderful. To tell you the truth, I hadn't given Thanksgiving much thought."

"It's this Thursday, you know." Spence held Jessie's coat as she slipped it on. "Do you think you can make it?"

"As far as I know, we don't have any plans. It would be hard for Gram and me to spend Thanksgiving alone at the house." Jessie's voice caught with emotion at the thought of the empty holiday season.

They walked outside to wait for Jessie's cab. Snow had begun to fall. The air was filled with fat white flakes, and a light sparkling blanket covered the sidewalk where they stood. The traffic noise was muffled as the snowfall hushed the familiar sounds of car engines and honking horns.

Spence and Jessie stood huddled close together as they waited by the curb.

"I'm sorry I can't see you to your door, Jessie. I hope you don't mind terribly."

Jessie smiled into his concerned eyes. "I don't mind at all. I'm glad you're the kind of man that has such a commitment to your patients . . . the kind of doctor, I should say. I'll be just fine in a cab."

The taxi honked its arrival as the driver pulled up to the curb. Spence held the back door open for Jessie. While she got in, he leaned into the front window on the passenger side and gave the driver Jessie's address and a 20 dollar bill.

"Keep the change," he instructed the driver.

Before he closed Jessie's door, he bent over to say goodnight. "I hope I'll be seeing you Thursday, Jessie. I enjoyed being with you tonight."

"I had a good time, too, Spence. Thank you."

Spence pushed her door shut, and the cab pulled away. Jessie turned and looked out the back window. He was standing in the snow, watching as the cab slowly disappeared into the white night.

6
· · · · ·

*T*HREE GENTLE RAPS on the oak door wakened Jessie from a sound sleep. A shaft of morning sunlight fell across her blanket warming her bed, and she stretched lazily.

"Come in," she called cheerfully. Gram peered around the corner of the door. "Why, you were still sleeping, honey," she said. "I wouldn't have wakened you if I'd known."

"It's all right, Gram." Jessie yawned and patted the rumpled coverlet. "Come sit by me."

She saw that Gram welcomed the invitation. The older woman's enthusiasm made Jessie feel like a teenager again, giggling and full of secrets, ready to share the details of a special evening, just as she always had with her mother.

"He's quite a wonderful man, isn't he." For Gram it was a statement, not a question.

Jessie closed her eyes and remembered Spence's face last night as they parted. For an instant as he leaned into the cab, Jessie thought he would kiss her. Jessie opened her eyes and answered Gram in a dreamy voice. "I've never known anyone so . . . so . . ."

"Unwavering?" Gram finished the sentence.

"Yes!" Jessie sat straight up in bed at this new thought. "Unwavering. Spence is so sure of who he is. Sure of what he wants. He doesn't vacillate between right and wrong like so many of the men I've known."

"Spencer is at peace with himself," Gram said firmly. "And that, Jessie, is exactly why I don't want you to get your

41

hopes up about this relationship. He is a determined man with an unshakable sense of values that he is not likely to compromise for any woman who doesn't share them."

Surprised at the tone of her grandmother's voice, Jessie stared at Gram blankly and sank back into the pillows on her bed.

"You see, Jessie," Gram continued, "I have known Spencer McCord and his family for many years. Since the day his father died when Spence was 10 years old, he has wanted nothing more than to be a physician. The doctor we had in town back then was up in years and liked to . . . well . . . frankly, he was a drunk. Mr. McCord was in a farming accident . . . they sent little Spencer to bring help, but the doctor was nowhere to be found. The child pounded on Doc Long's door for 30 minutes before he finally shinnied through a window and found the doctor on his couch, passed out with a hangover. By the time Spencer and the doctor returned to the farm, it was too late. Mr. McCord bled to death."

Spence's father died because of the neglect of an alcoholic doctor. Jessie was stunned. No wonder he had told her last night that he knew what hate could do.

"How bitter he must be!" She whispered the words to Gram.

"Bitter?" Gram said, surprised. "Hardly, child. There is no room for bitterness in a man like Spencer McCord."

Jessie sat silent and Gram paused. "And there is no room in his future for a wife either, I'm afraid," she finished softly. "I've heard him mention many times that to ask any woman to share his life-style would be unfair."

"That," Jessie said archly, "would depend on the woman."

"Perhaps. But, Jessie, Spencer's commitment to medicine is superceded by one other—his commitment to God. He is a very devout man."

The Bible. The worn brown leather Bible on Spence's old chair. Suddenly Jessie could think of nothing else. What was it she'd seen marked? *I will keep him in perfect peace whose mind is stayed on thee.* What interesting words. What an interesting man.

"Well, you can be sure I'm not in love with him or any man," Jessie said firmly to Gram. "I've got plenty of more important things to think about right now."

"Which reminds me," said Gram. "Uncle Charles called. He wants to come and talk business with you. He'll be your best ally and your strongest asset in running the newspaper. You'll need to depend on him heavily."

"Depend on him!" Jessie spoke vehemently. "I won't depend on him for any kind of help. I hate him."

Gram rose slowly from the bed and moved to the window. The morning sun had climbed since the two women began talking. She now stood in its path, which shone directly through the glass in a straight shaft of light. For a long time she didn't speak.

When she finally did turn to Jessie, her eyes brimming with tears, Gram's voice was more firm than Jessie had ever heard it.

"Jessie, Charles is my son—the only son I have now. I won't allow you to speak of him that way. He is a good man." Gram's hands were fisted at her sides. "Trust me, Jessie. He's a good Christian man . . . and he's my son." Gram's voice broke.

Jessie started out of bed, but Gram's hand waved her back. The older woman left the room without a word, and Jessie listened to her footsteps that moved more quickly than usual down the silent hallway.

Alone again, Jessie impatiently pulled the eyelet coverlet to the head of the bed. What a mess I've made of things, she thought. Obviously Gram didn't know Charles loved Lynn. Jessie was sure his clever scheming had kept his mother from realizing that he had ruined Philip's career as well. And now, his manufactured grief was fooling Gram again and driving a wedge between her and Jessie.

Despite her rage at Charles, Jessie was almost as angry with herself. She should know better than to hurt her grandmother the way she had. Somehow she must think of a way to right the wrong.

Jessie walked to the paned window and gave the casing a hard push. It opened reluctantly. She braced her hands on the sill and leaned out. The cold air slapped her face as she studied the flower bed and the old porch swing.

Jessie's fingers were stiff with the chill when she heard the sound of a car on the gravel driveway. Hurst didn't bark his usual alert as when a stranger came to call; Jessie knew it could only be Charles. She pulled her head in the window. "I can deal with this," she determined in her heart. She remembered Spence and his breath on her cheek. She remembered Gram's voice on the phone that day in the newsroom. "I *will* deal with this," she said aloud to the empty room. "I will."

Gram and Charles were sitting at the table drinking tea when Jessie walked purposefully into the kitchen. "Good morning, Charles," she said cheerfully. Kissing her grandmother's forehead she passed by the table and disappeared into the pantry.

"Mind if I join you? I need a cup of coffee this morning. Something a bit stronger than tea. At least that's what the Californians say." Her voice filtered out of the pantry. She reappeared with the coffee canister under one arm. "I still drink it with plenty of cream though." She hastily glanced at Gram and Charles.

Gram looked relieved, and Charles was smiling broadly at her. Jessie felt a surge of strength—perhaps Gram had told him nothing.

"Plenty of cream," Charles was saying, pushing the china pitcher toward her. "Any good New Englander has to have plenty of cream."

Jessie positioned herself at the table, sitting next to Gram and opposite Charles. "Gram tells me you have some business matters to discuss," she said. Jessie hoped Gram noticed the extra effort she was putting into this conversation.

As if in answer to Jessie's thoughts, Gram reached her thin arm around the younger woman's shoulder and gave her a quick squeeze. "Let me leave you two alone. I never did understand these 'business matters' as you call them."

Knowing that Gram managed the books for Grandfather's newspaper for years, Jessie stole a quick look at Charles. His amused expression, so like her father's, spoke for itself.

Gram's tactics certainly became more transparent with her age.

The older woman stood quickly and began clearing the teacups. As Gram moved to the kitchen counter behind Jessie's seat, the crash of china in the porcelain sink shattered the stillness of the kitchen. Charles was at his mother's side before Jessie could get out of her chair. She turned just in time to see Gram sway into his arms.

For an instant, Jessie thought the older woman had fainted. But Gram, though leaning heavily on her son, was mumbling faintly. "Oh, forgive me. I guess I'm a little dizzy this morning. Now look at my good china . . . all broken into pieces. I'll clean it up . . . I'll clean it up right away."

Gram was still talking as Jessie and Charles helped her to the bed in the first-floor guest room. Her protests quieted as Charles insisted she lay on the burgundy and blue quilted comforter. Gram reached out a hand to Jessie and pulled her to a seat on the side of the bed. She traced the design on one of the quilt squares with her first finger as she spoke.

"Did you know I made this quilt for your mother, Jessie? It was her wedding present—hers and Philip's. Lynn never put it on her own bed. She saved it for her guests. She said it made her guest room the prettiest room in the house."

Jessie stroked Gram's forehead, smoothing back her hair over and over again with her hand. "I know, Gram. I know." She bent tenderly over the older woman. "Do you remember the day I got spanked for jumping on this very bed?"

Gram laughed and Jessie noticed the color returning to her face. "Indeed, I do," she said, "you were such a tomboy." Her voice grew stronger. "Now really, I must get up and take care of that broken china."

"You'll rest this morning," said Charles firmly, "while I call Dr. McCord. You told me you didn't sleep well last night. I'm quite sure fatigue contributed to your feeling faint."

"Why didn't you sleep well?" Jessie asked.

Gram looked sheepish. "I was wondering about your date," she said lamely, glaring at Charles. "And as for calling Spencer, don't bother. I will call him myself."

That same amused look Jessie had seen at the breakfast table crossed Charles' face. Jessie giggled, and Gram motioned impatiently. "Go on, now. You have work to do."

Charles went first, and with a glance over her shoulder at Gram, who looked a bit chagrined, Jessie followed, shutting the door softly behind her.

7

•••••

*I*T WAS THE FIRST TIME Jessie had been in church since the funeral of her parents. For three weeks Gram had urged her to come, and each Sunday Jessie had manufactured an excuse. This Sunday she had reached the end of her creativity, and Gram wouldn't take no for an answer.

Jessie had to admit there was something almost supernatural about the peace in this place. She sat on the old wooden pews, dark and smooth with age, waiting for the service to begin. The small sanctuary, stone on the outside and mortar on the inside, hushed the sounds of the world beyond its doors. Muted light filtered through the brilliant reds and violets of the stained-glass windows. Covered with white linen, the Communion table sat on a platform just beyond the altar, solemn and resplendent. Jessie closed her eyes as she waited, sensing the peace around her and fighting the turmoil within her.

The peal of a pipe organ, much too large for the small sanctuary, interrupted Jessie's introspection. The organist, whoever she was, was a fine musician. The strains of "How Great Thou Art" echoed majestically off the high ceiling. As the choir began to file in, Jessie watched the pretty blond woman at the organ curiously. Her face was radiant, and her fingers fairly flew over the keyboard as she played the old hymn. Jessie guessed the organist to be close to her own age. What would such a talented musician be doing in a church as small as this? She would be sure to ask Gram about it later.

As the prelude concluded Jessie looked over the congregation. She didn't see Spence, but knew from her conversations with Gram that he never missed a service. He must be on call at the hospital, she thought with a twinge of disappointment. Seeing him was the only bright spot in coming here this morning. She certainly wouldn't be gaining any great insights from the pastor, Rev. Rogers. Jessie's only contact with him was at the funeral, and though he was well-meaning, his conversation rambled too much to suit her.

A sudden movement at the side door of the sanctuary caught Jessie's eye. Her heart lurched as Spence and Charles entered the church, intent in conversation. The two stood for a moment, then shook hands and parted. Spence climbed the three steps to the platform and sat down. Jessie scooted lower in her seat. "Don't see me, Charles," she whispered under her breath. "Please, don't see me."

"What?" Gram leaned closer to Jessie.

"Nothing, Gram."

"Why, there's Charles!" Gram whispered. She raised a thin hand and waved in the direction of her son, who was obviously looking over the congregation in hopes of finding his mother. Smiling broadly to acknowledge Gram's wave, Charles started back toward them. Jessie pasted on a smile and began to study the printed Order of Worship with renewed fervor.

The service began just as Charles slipped into his seat beside Gram. By the time he reached across his mother's lap to squeeze Jessie's hand, she had practically memorized the morning agenda. A call to worship, two songs (pages 135 and 267 in the red hymnal) and a welcome to the visitors. The scripture lesson would be read by Spencer McCord. Jessie smiled stiffly at Charles, bowed her head, and pretended to pray.

During the customary welcome to visitors, Jessie stood, taking care to smile at all the kind faces she remembered from the funeral. She knew Gram was proud of her and was glad she came today. Spence watched her from the chancel; Jessie could feel his admiration despite the distance between them.

When the time came for the scripture reading, Spence stood in the pulpit, gazing seriously over the congregation. "Let us stand for this reading of the Word of God." Jessie watched his face.

"The Scripture reading for the morning hour is taken from the Book of Psalms, chapter 30, verses 4 and 5." Spence's voice was strong and clear.

> *"Sing to the Lord, you saints of his;*
> *praise his holy name.*
> *For his anger lasts only a moment,*
> *but his favor lasts a lifetime;*
> *weeping may remain for a night,*
> *but rejoicing comes in the morning"* (NIV).

Hot tears stung Jessie's eyes. Would she ever rejoice again? Feelings Jessie didn't understand stirred deep within her.

As the pastor approached the pulpit, Jessie saw Spence exit through the chancel door. He would be on his way to the hospital.

Jessie listened with interest as the pastor began his message. He didn't ramble nearly as much as she had expected, but midway through, her mind began to wander. She was reviewing yesterday's conversation with Charles about the state of Dad's affairs when Gram unexpectedly clasped her hand. As the older woman dabbed her eyes with her lace hankie, Jessie tried to regroup. Rev. Rogers must be saying something Gram wanted Jessie to hear.

". . . several in our midst who have experienced much weeping in recent months."

Jessie stiffened at the pastor's words. Surely he wouldn't single out her and Gram. She looked away from the pulpit, avoiding any eye contact with Rev. Rogers. No, she thought in relief a few moments later—he wasn't going to mention her name. Jessie relaxed and listened more closely.

". . . God loves you," the Reverend said sincerely. "He understands your grief. And the way you yearn for loved ones who have been lost to you is the way God yearns for you to be His child."

The same stirrings Jessie felt earlier in the morning resurfaced. Maybe God understood her predicament after all.

By this time, Gram's handkerchief was soaked. Jessie rummaged in her purse, found a tissue, and handed it to Gram. Charles sat with his arm draped around his mother's shoulders. His attentiveness to Gram distracted Jessie. She wished he would just disappear from their lives.

When the service ended, Gram and Charles started down the center aisle to the vestibule. Jessie looked around desperately. She must figure out a way to avoid standing in this long line of people with Charles. Quickly she tapped Gram's shoulder.

"I'm going to talk with the organist, Gram."

"Oh, honey, she's a delightful person . . ." Not waiting for Gram to finish her reply, Jessie started up the aisle against the sea of people. When she finally reached the front, the young woman at the organ was placing the last of her sheet music in a large satchel.

"You play beautifully." Jessie smiled and stretched out her hand. Now that she was closer, she could see that the tiny blond woman had a very pretty face and unusually blue eyes.

"Thank you. God has been gracious to me." She smiled back at Jessie as she clasped her hand warmly. "I'm Nicole Clark—and you're Jessie Sterling."

"Yes. How did you know?"

"Let's just say we have a mutual friend." Nicole's eyes sparkled. "I've been wanting to meet you," she continued without giving Jessie a chance to inquire about the "mutual friend."

"I was so sorry to hear about the death of your parents. I wanted to come to their funeral, but it was too soon for me. You see, my own husband died about eight months ago. It's still very hard."

"I'm sorry." Jessie liked this woman's honesty.

"Thank you. The pastor talked this morning about 'weeping enduring for the night and joy coming in the morning.'

I'm just beginning to understand what that scripture means. Maybe we could get together sometime?"

"I'd like that." Jessie was pleased at the prospect.

"Great! Excuse me now—I have to go pick up my son, Josh. He's in the nursery. These services can get long for the little guy. It was such a pleasure to meet you, Jessie. I'll pray for you."

"Thanks," Jessie called as Nicole left for the nursery. She felt certain she'd made a new friend.

8

•••••

*T*HE LAST EMBERS of what had been a roaring fire popped and crackled in the fireplace as Jessie scratched Hurst's velvety ears. The old house was chilly, and Jessie had positioned the setter on top of her stockinged feet to warm them. Now she spoke softly into the dog's sleepy face, which she cradled in her hand.

"Who would think running a weekly newspaper could be so difficult, Hurst? How did we merit the good fortune to be born in a newspaper family? And how am I ever, ever going to get out of this mess?" Jessie sighed, picked up her nearly empty coffee cup, and headed toward the kitchen. Hurst followed obediently, stepping on a few of the stacks of papers that were strewn in disarray around the room.

Jessie, clad in her sweats, walked quickly across the cold wooden floor to the sink. As she reached for the faucet handle to rinse her cup, she felt a prick in the ball of her foot. Jessie knew instantly it must be a piece of china from the cup Gram had broken Saturday morning. She yanked a chair from the table, sat down and pulled off her sock to examine the damage. An expanding dot of blood stained her sock and her foot, but try as she might, Jessie could not see the sliver of glass.

The sound of the doorbell interrupted her search. Jessie started as the noise echoed through the still house. Grabbing Hurst by the collar she limped toward the door. Who would be calling at this hour? She flipped on the porch light and peered out. Spencer McCord. Jessie gasped and her hand went to her hair. How silly she must look, standing here with her hair a mess, one sock off and the other on, in her oldest pair of sweats. She felt a sudden urge to turn off the light and pretend she wasn't home. But of course, Spence knew she was here, and despite her embarrassment, Jessie was glad. Besides, she had always had the ability to laugh at herself, and so, with a wry smile, she opened the door.

A gust of wind and a flurry of blowing snow ushered him in. "Spence, what are you doing out this time of night?" Jessie looked up into his hazel eyes and was surprised at the light that seemed to flicker in them when he looked at her. She had the unassured feeling she'd experienced at their first meeting, and her heart was pounding."

"Take my coat and I'll tell you about it," he said, grinning easily at her.

Disconcerted by her own lack of hospitality and his teasing, Jessie forgot about her foot and stepped toward him. As she did, the elusive glass pricked her again, and she flinched, wincing in pain and losing her balance. Spence caught her and the wet roughness of his overcoat pressed against her face. Without warning she was supported by his arms, neither of them anxious to move apart.

"Jessie, are you hurt?" His voice sounded hoarse. Was it emotion or the surprise of the moment? Surely he didn't think she'd purposely fallen into his arms.

Jessie struggled to right herself. "It's my foot. . . ." She looked up at him. It was so hard to think with his face this close to hers.

Spence scooped her up and carried her to the overstuffed chair by the fireplace. Lowering her gently into its cushions, he took off his overcoat and threw it over the back of the chair. Droplets from the melted snowflakes spattered Jessie on the face.

His eyes were on her foot, and as he dropped to one knee he cradled it gingerly in his hand. "What seems to be the trouble here?" The gruffness in his voice was gone.

As Jessie related the story of Gram and the teacups, Spence frowned his concern but refrained from comment. When she concluded, he turned her foot under the brass floor lamp standing by the chair.

"Let's take a look at this glass. Oh, yes, there it is." Spence got up quickly and disappeared into the hall bathroom. Jessie could hear him rummaging through the medicine cabinet and then the vanity drawers. Eventually he emerged with a pair of tweezers and a bottle of rubbing alcohol.

"An old home remedy, I presume?" Jessie said lightly as Spence knelt again by her chair.

He lifted her foot carefully. "Now this may sting a little, so be patient."

Jessie winced as Spence made an unsuccessful attempt to grasp the glass with the tweezers. "Couldn't we just let this work its way out—like a splinter?" she asked through gritted teeth.

Spence's look reprimanded her. "There's a funny thing about a splinter. It seems so small and insignificant. Yet left untreated, it causes a lot of pain . . ." Spence paused but never lifted his head from his work. "That's the way it is with a person's heart, too, Jessie. The smallest bitterness left to fester will cause an undue share of heartache."

"Ouch!" Jessie jerked her foot out of Spence's grasp.

Triumphantly he held the tweezers with the fragment of glass for her to see. "I got it!" he grinned boyishly. Spence dabbed the alcohol on her foot with a cotton ball and covered the spot with a Band-Aid.

Jessie relaxed in her chair. "Thanks. This turned out to be quite a providential house call."

Spence laughed warmly. "It was my pleasure." His directness made Jessie's cheeks go pink.

"Now that I'm in a better condition to be a hostess, let me clear you a place to sit." Jessie began shuffling the papers spread over the couch.

"Interesting," Spence said as he surveyed the mess. "I believe they call this 'organized clutter.'" He was teasing Jessie about the comment she'd made at his apartment, and she loved it.

"Actually, no." She laughed. "It's the very disorganized financial records of Dad's paper. I can't make much out of them yet. I've been reviewing the books all day." Her smile faded. ". . . but let's not talk about that. What *are* you doing out at . . . ," as Jessie looked at the clock on the mantle her face registered surprise, ". . . one o'clock in the morning?"

"Is it *that* late?" Spence groaned, and Jessie noticed that the tiny lines around his eyes seemed especially pronounced. How many hours had he worked today she wondered.

"Nicole Clark brought her baby into the emergency room about 10:30 this evening. The child's temperature was high. Nicole thought he might have pneumonia. The baby was fine, but I didn't want them to drive home alone in this weather. I followed her and noticed your lights on. Thought I'd stop in and see if you and your grandmother were OK. He motioned to her foot. Looks like it's a good thing I did."

Yes, indeed, Jessie thought, smiling as she studied his face from veiled lashes. It was a very good thing he did.

*   *   *

Jessie leaned against the door jam long after Spence's taillights disappeared down the dark road. She peered through the blinds on the adjoining window watching the snow float down in the glow of the yard light beside the gravel drive. If the snow didn't stop soon, she'd never make it to the newsroom in the morning. At the moment, she didn't care much. Something about Spence's visit had seemed to alleviate her anxiety and quiet her restless spirit. What was it about him that was so settling?

Her thoughts drifted to Nicole Clark and her baby. How kind of Spence to follow them home in this weather. After church last week, Jessie had asked Gram more about the pretty young organist. It seemed Nicole was Gram's nearest neighbor, more than a mile down the road. She was a young widow, whose husband had been dead less than a year. Gram couldn't recall what killed him; an illness of some sort, she'd said. Jessie remembered thinking it was odd Gram would forget such an important detail.

Jessie drew a sharp breath—could Spence's trip to the Clark home signal more than an interest in the baby? Abruptly Jessie let go of the blinds, and they clattered against the windowpane. So much for musings on the snowstorm. What if Spence had more than a friendly interest in Nicole—suddenly she was sure it was true. Her heart sank, and the peace she was feeling melted away like the white flakes on the floor of Gram's entrance hall.

And what if he does? Jessie thought angrily, making her way back to the document-laden couch. She certainly didn't have any claim on Spence. Why should she be upset—and besides, Gram had warned her about this. Maybe Gram had known all the time that Spence was seeing someone else.

Jessie bent over the coffee table impatiently and began shuffling through the stack of papers, not even sure what she was looking for. In her haste, she didn't notice the bottle of rubbing alcohol perched on the table's edge. Over it went, uncapped, running down the side of Jessie's leg onto her sore foot. Jessie retrieved a kitchen towel and began soaking up the mess. As she worked on her hands and knees, Hurst who was undaunted by the smell, enthusiastically covered Jessie's face with sloppy wet kisses.

"Stop, Hurst! Get down!" Jessie covered her face with both arms. What more could happen in one evening? Suddenly the hilarity of the situation struck her. As quickly as it came, Jessie's frustration vanished. She collapsed to the floor and rolled to her back, laughing heartily as she buried her face in the dog's red fur.

* * *

Morning found Jessie still in her clothes, asleep on the couch. When she awoke Gram was sitting patiently in the chair opposite her, holding a cup of tea and studying her carefully.

"Hi." Jessie bent her stiff neck from side to side.

"Jessica, you're not getting enough rest, and that's all

there is to it." Gram's pronouncement sounded like the beginning of a lecture, so Jessie righted herself quickly and forced a smile.

"It's nothing, Gram. I worked late—that's all."

Gram would not be put off. "Nonsense. It's stress and I know it. Undue stress can cause health problems—even in someone your age."

"You sound just like Spence," Jessie muttered between yawns. More distinctly she answered, "It's just work, Gram. I have a lot to consider at the paper, you know."

"I'm quite sure your father's business is financially stable. It always has been. How else do you think he could live this well?" Gram's arm made a wide sweep as she gestured around the stately old living room.

Jessie hesitated. How much should she tell the older woman?

"Gram, *The Courier* is in trouble. Real trouble. Dad had been meeting the payroll from his reserves for more than a year. *The Courier* has been operating in the red at least that long."

"Are you sure? He never alluded to anything of the sort . . . and why wouldn't he let me know . . ." Gram's voice trailed into silence.

"Face it," Jessie said flatly. "Dad was fighting a losing battle. With the increases in the cost of newsprint and the price of new technology, an operation as small as his hardly stands a chance. And you know he was always committed to pay his employees top dollar. How can a local weekly compete against a daily as large as Charles'? It's a safe bet Dad would rather go bankrupt than to dismiss his senior employees one by one. Some of those people have been with *The Courier* since Dad started it."

Jessie hadn't intended to say so much, especially in the light of Gram's recent fainting episode. She should shield her grandmother from the painful realities. Jessie anxiously patted Gram's arm as she headed for the stairs up to her room.

"I've made it sound much worse than it is," she said cheerfully. "What this paper needs is some young blood. Actually, I've got several ideas for orchestrating a comeback. Charles gave me some very practical insights."

"Oh?" said Gram brightly. "What did he . . . ?"

"Sorry, no time to talk now," Jessie interrupted from the top of the landing. "I need to be at the office early to start on the new strategies."

Without waiting for a reply, Jessie shut her bedroom door behind her, taking a deep breath as she leaned on it. Her fingers were still crossed behind her back.

Jessie was grateful for the good weather as she drove to the newsroom that morning. The weatherman had predicted this break in the storm system but forecast more snow for late afternoon. Much longer around the house and she would have been faced with more questions from Gram—questions she couldn't answer. A nagging guilt preoccupied her. Why had she told Gram she had plans of "orchestrating a comeback"? It couldn't have been further from the truth.

Only Saturday morning, Charles and she had reviewed the grim facts over coffee at the dining room table. There was no salvaging the paper, he'd said. The finances were hopeless. Bankruptcy was the only viable option. Why didn't she just sell *The Courier* to him? He would remunerate her generously and be sure all the employees were treated fairly. Jessie recoiled at the thought. She would never betray her father by selling out to his conniving twin! The tide of bitterness within Jessie swelled strong, and waves of nausea washed over her. She stopped the car on the side of the road and rested her head on the steering wheel. Her insides felt as ugly and tangled as the early morning deposit of seaweed on a California beach.

When the nausea passed, Jessie pulled the car back on the road. Perhaps there *was* something to this notion that unresolved anger would cause more grief than it was worth. Never mind, Jessie told herself, Charles was not worthy to be forgiven. She would prove him wrong and find a way to salvage *The Courier.*

As Jessie pulled into the small parking lot, she renewed her resolve to make something of Dad's paper. She wouldn't let him down, not after all he'd done for her. After turning off the ignition, she sat for a moment, studying the shabby building before her. The once beautiful red brick was in disrepair. What had been gleaming white guttering showed signs of pulling away from its mooring. The cracked and peeling front door was the victim of one too many poor paint jobs. Even the asphalt in the parking lot had buckled under the strain of so many hard years.

Despite all this, Jessie loved the place. As she walked through the door into the newsroom, she felt a surge of exhilaration. These were her roots. This place was her heritage. Here, on an old manual Olivetti, she had typed her first story about the local elementary school carnival. And with careful attention from a helpful copy editor, Dad had published it. The incident had precipitated her ongoing love affair with the printed page.

This day the newsroom bustled with activity, as usual. The staff, engrossed in jobs completely familiar to them, scarcely looked up when the door banged behind her. "Hello, Jess," called Joe Fischer as he wandered out of the typesetting room. "I've got to fix the spring on that door ... hasn't shut right for two years. Your dad said not to bother, said it's so noisy in here we needed the bang for a doorbell."

"It's OK, Mr. Fischer." Jessie smiled at the old man as she added her jacket to those piled on a chair in the corner. "If it's good enough for Dad, it's good enough for me." The old man grinned and saluted with an ink-smudged hand.

Jessie slowly surveyed the newsroom. Despite her years of experience she hardly knew where to begin. They don't need me here, she thought.

Lacy Thompson should be the managing editor ... she'd been with Dad 28 years and done everything but get her name on the first line of the masthead. And James Perry, a local, middle-aged man with a family, was the copy chief. He certainly wasn't planning to make a career move after 13 years with *The Courier*. The same thing was true for the handful of other employees. Even the summer intern from a nearby college had stayed on into the autumn. The group could put out the paper very well without her. It seemed a little presumptuous to come in and change things. Did these people know their futures were on the line, Jessie wondered. In her effort to save them, would she become their enemy?

She walked quickly to James' desk. "Where are we?"

"We've just about put her to bed," he answered. "I've still got an eight-column inch hole to fill on the op-ed page, though. Mr. Sterling usually did that spread . . . there are some wire-service stories over there." He gestured toward the layout table next to Lacy Thompson's desk.

Jessie made her way to the table and leafed quickly through the stack. She chose a UPI editorial and picked up a blue pencil. From the corner of her eye Jessie noticed Lacy watching. She approached the older woman's desk.

"Hi, Mrs. Thompson," she said cautiously.

"I'm going over the books, Jessie." Mrs. Thompson peered at Jessie over the top of her spectacles. "They aren't good." Lacy tapped the red vinyl ledger with the eraser on her pencil. "Not good at all."

"I know," said Jessie quietly.

"Our reserves are almost gone."

"I know."

"In two months we won't be able to meet our payroll."

"I know."

Jessie looked at her friend desperately. "What would Dad have done?"

Tears filled Mrs. Thompson's eyes. "I don't know, honey," she said, placing her hand over Jessie's. "I wish I did."

9
· · · · ·

A FRESH BLANKET OF SNOW covered the night as Jessie, attaché case under one arm, made her way to the car. She had stayed at the office later than she had planned. Almost 10 P.M. Gram would already be in bed.

The windshield was snow-covered. Jessie opened the door on the driver's side and tossed her attaché case and purse onto the far side of the front seat, looking to no avail on the floor of the car, front and back, for an ice scraper. Her gloved hand would have to do.

Getting back out of the car, she slammed the driver's door shut, dislodging some of the wet snow, which splatted coldly on the tops of both her feet.

Grimly, Jessie began to clear the back windshield. Her feet were cold; she was tired; and now the deceptively beautiful snow showed itself to be a most unpleasant slush, numbing her hands right through her gloves.

Jessie got back in the car, started the engine, and turned the defroster to high. With a little luck, the windshield wipers would take care of the front windshield.

She was right. The wipers sent the icy mixture sliding wetly to the sides of the windshield. She stripped off her soaked gloves and tossed them on the floor in front of the passenger's seat.

Pulling slowly out of the parking lot onto the street, Jessie was relieved to see that the traffic had kept the streets mostly cleared of snow, but wet. Smiling wryly, she promised herself to remember this weather if she ever had the chance to return to California.

I hope it doesn't get colder tonight, she thought. If the roads get much worse it might be tough getting out to Mrs. McCord's for Thanksgiving dinner tomorrow. She was looking forward to spending the day with Spence at his mother's farm.

Pulling into the gravel drive, Jessie glanced up at the dark house. If Mom and Dad were here, the windows would be ablaze. She supposed they had never gone to bed before midnight in their lives. The familiar ache passed slowly through her throat.

Jessie parked behind the house in the carport and went in through the back door onto the enclosed porch. Once inside, she slipped off her shoes and dropped her purse and briefcase on the floor. Taking off her damp coat, she threw it over the chest freezer that hummed softly in the corner and hurried into the warm kitchen.

Gram had left the light on over the sink, and it cast long shadows over the large kitchen. Jessie didn't turn on another light but walked straight to the refrigerator and opened the door wide. Reaching for an apple while she continued to search for something more substantial, she detected the sound of movement in another part of the house and stood up straight, closing the refrigerator door. It wasn't footsteps she heard, yet something . . . the swinging door that separated the kitchen from the rest of the house suddenly swung open and Hurst padded onto the wooden floor. Excited at seeing Jessie, he wagged his tail so vigorously that his entire posterior moved ridiculously from side to side, and his half-open mouth grinned at her with silly delight.

Jessie knelt down and pulled him to her. Burying her face in his furry neck, she laughed with relief.

"Hurst, you scared me to death." Jessie scratched him behind his ears and patted his wet nose, then stood and walked through the enclosed porch to let him out. She was sure he'd be ready to come in before she was finished eating.

Jessie turned on the kitchen light and resumed her search of the refrigerator. Finding ham already sliced, Jessie stacked that, along with cheese and mustard, onto wheat bread and added a handful of chips. With a glass of milk and her sandwich, she sat down at the kitchen table and finished off her late supper in a matter of minutes.

The oak chair scraped annoyingly across the floor as she stood and scooted it back with her legs. After carrying her dishes to the sink, she called Hurst in, locked the doors, and climbed the steps to her room.

Gram's door was closed, and no sliver of light showed underneath, so Jessie decided not to chance disturbing her to say goodnight. She headed down the hall to her own bedroom, peeling off her sweater on the way. She walked to her bedside table and turned on the small lamp, threw her sweater across the back of the side chair, and stepped out of her skirt. Crossing to the small bathroom, Jessie turned the water on in the shower and stepped into the steamy warmth. The hot water was revitalizing to her tired bones, and she splashed some onto her face before soaping herself and rinsing. She was in the shower less than five minutes but felt refreshed and pulled on her robe. Maybe she'd get her briefcase off the back porch and look through a few more of Dad's files before she went to sleep.

When Jessie came back into her room, Hurst was lying on the foot of her bed, but his neck was erect, his head cocked, his ears pitched toward the ceiling.

"What's the matter, boy?" Jessie looked toward her bedroom door where Hurst was staring. "Did you hear something?"

Jessie froze, her hairbrush posed next to her ear. She didn't hear anything, and Hurst laid his big head back comfortably on his paws, heaving a noisy sigh.

She was opening her bedroom door to go retrieve her briefcase from the back porch when she distinctly heard a muffled banging sound downstairs, coming from the direction of the front door. As she stepped cautiously into the hall, Hurst brushed against her legs as he bounded for the stairs, a

guttural, growling sound emitting from his shadow as he trot-
ted toward the front door.

Hurst was sitting by the door when she arrived and
peeked through the small windowpane. She flipped on the
porch light. Nothing.

Jessie opened the door slowly, "Is someone there?"

Hurst whined plaintively to be allowed out.

"No, boy, you're staying with me," Jessie whispered.

Pulling the door open wide now, Jessie pushed on the
storm door.

"Stay."

She pushed the storm door open wide enough to allow
her to stick her head out. There was no one there—no strange
sounds. She was beginning to feel silly, yet she was certain
Hurst had heard what she had. Maybe the wind . . .

Squinting to see through the snow into the front yard,
Jessie's blood suddenly turned as cold as the icy pellets blowing against her face. Footprints . . . from the bottom step of
the porch toward the east side of the house. Were her eyes
playing tricks? They were so faint . . . yet the blowing snow
wouldn't leave them undisturbed for long. Clutching her robe
at her throat, Jessie scrambled through the living room into
the dining room, where the large window would give her a
clear view of the driveway.

No car was parked there, but with a sinking feeling, she
realized the tracks her car had made when she drove in had
disappeared. No doubt . . . the footprints in front of the house
were fresh.

Should she wake Gram . . . call the police?

Suddenly, Hurst's frantic barking split the darkness inside
the house. Jessie heard a low, frightened groan escape from
her throat. Hurst loped past her toward the back porch. Jessie
followed him into the kitchen.

She could hear the banging sound at the back door now.
Her left hand secured her white terrycloth robe around her as
her right hand clamped tightly across her own mouth.

Jessie moved slowly through the kitchen. When she
reached the door, she peered across the enclosed porch to the

64

outside door. She could distinctly see the outline of a large man's form. Hurst was running in place at her side, barking loudly, his presence and size lending her courage. She opened the door that separated the kitchen and porch.

"Who's there? What do you want?" She stepped quickly across the porch to get a better look, not thinking of the flimsiness of the hook-lock that separated her from the figure looming there. One quick jerk of his wrist and the intruder was on the porch beside her.

She sensed him before she could make out his features in the dim light.

Suddenly his arms were around her, as she was enveloped in his familiar scent and the smoothness of his cheek against hers. The sound of her own name was echoing crazily amid Hurst's persistent barking.

"Jessie, Jessie . . ."

"It's all right, it's all right," Jessie mumbled softly into his shoulder. "It's all right."

None of the three shadows on the porch knew if she was reassuring Hurst, Brad, or herself.

✳ ✳ ✳

The big Irish setter eyed Brad suspiciously as he and Jessie, arm in arm, proceeded into the kitchen.

"Why didn't you tell me you were coming? If I had a gun in the house, I might have shot you. How did you get here?—there's no car."

"I decided a couple of weeks ago to get a ticket. I was afraid to wait until too close to the holiday weekend—thought the flights might all be booked solid. No way I was gonna spend Thanksgiving without you. Then I took a cab out here from Boston. Cost me an arm and a leg."

His eyes followed Jessie as she put on a pot of coffee. Sleep would wait.

"Where's your grandma?"

"Gram's already in bed. She goes to bed pretty early these days. I don't think she's been up to par since Mom and Dad died."

"How are you, Jess? Are you handling things OK?"

Jessie smiled. "The pain is easing. But, I miss them so much. It's not that I spent so much time with them since I've been grown, but they were always there—I thought they always would be."

Brad pulled out a chair and sat down at the table.

"The coffee will be ready in a few minutes. Are you hungry? Can I get you anything?"

She could hardly keep her eyes from his face. How could she have forgotten how handsome he was! His boyish features were perfectly chiseled and bronzed from the California sun. His blue eyes reflected his admiration for her as he filled her in on the lives of their mutual friends in California. He had seen Sarah . . . she sent Jessie her love.

Hurst watched silently, sitting on the floor not far from them. Alertly, he watched Brad as he spoke, then Jessie, then Brad again. His head turned first toward one, then the other, as if watching a tennis match.

"Is your grandma fixing dinner here tomorrow?"

Jessie gulped. She hadn't yet thought of what Brad's being here would mean for their Thanksgiving plans.

"Dinner . . . well, no, actually. Uh, a friend of hers, well and of mine, too, for that matter . . . lives in the country . . . Mrs. McCord has invited us out to her farm to have dinner with her," and added almost inaudibly "and her son."

"You don't think it'll be a problem to have one more, do you?"

"Well, we'll let Gram call her in the morning. I don't know how we'll work it out." Jessie's voice trailed off, but her mind was spinning as she got out the cups and poured the coffee.

She was surprised at her delight in seeing Brad, but she had been so looking forward to seeing Spence again. There was no way that she could keep Brad and Spence apart. Mrs. McCord would insist they bring him along. Who ever heard of a Thanksgiving dinner that couldn't easily be stretched to serve one more?

Guiltily, she began making excuses to herself for being in

this predicament. She didn't owe Spence anything, and she had never committed herself to Brad. But she knew Brad had no idea that she had a flicker of interest in someone else. And she had unmistakenly told Spencer McCord that she had been seeing someone in California but that it was nothing serious. Now "nothing serious" had flown the length of the country to spend Thanksgiving with her—and Spence.

Frantically, she thought of feigning illness. But that would be hard to pull off with Spence a practicing physician and Brad serving his medical residency. Even if she did convince them she was ill, Gram would insist on taking Brad with her out to the farm, and Spence and Brad alone together would be worse than the three of them peering at each other over a stuffed turkey.

Jessie returned the coffeepot to its burner and set out the cream and sugar.

There was no way out—she would be having Thanksgiving dinner with Mrs. McCord, Gram, Spence, and Brad.

She sat down at the table with Brad and reached for the cream and sugar. As she began to absent-mindedly add the sugar to her coffee, Brad watched her intently.

"Do you have someplace here I could sleep tonight? I'll go to a hotel in the morning."

"Don't be silly. Gram would be mortified if you stay anywhere but here. We have a guest room that is always ready. I'll show you to it when we finish our coffee."

Brad smiled easily. "That's what I was hopin' you'd say."

Same old Brad, saying all the right things, trusting his charm to mesmerize everyone with whom he came in contact. Instead of slightly irritating Jessie as it had before she left California, it amused her. She knew what to expect from Brad. With everything in her life so uncertain right now, she found that comforting.

They sat quietly for a few minutes, drinking their coffee. Jessie was silently envisioning a worst case/best case scenario for dinner tomorrow.

Brad broke the silence. "Will you come back with me, Jess? Will you come back home with me?"

Surprised, Jessie looked at him sharply. "You know I can't do that."

"Why not? Life goes on. I want our lives to go on together—the way we'd planned."

"The way *you'd* planned. I'm just not ready yet. I've got things to settle at the paper, and I don't know if I could leave Gram just now."

"You can get your dad's lawyers or somebody to sell the paper for you. And your grandma's going to have to get used to you leaving sooner or later. You're not going to do her any good by babying her through this thing, Jess."

"What an unkind thing to say." Irritation was resurfacing, and Jessie's voice rose a pitch, reflecting her feelings. Hurst scooted forward slightly, watchful and alert.

"I'm sorry!" Brad said loudly, not sounding sorry at all. "I think I've been patient. You've been here for weeks. I miss you and want you to come back so we can get on with our lives. What's wrong with that?"

Jessie wasn't ready to cope with this. Her elbows on the table, she put her face in her hands.

"Brad, please. Surely, we're not going to fight about this the whole time you're here."

He realized he'd gone too far. He stood and reached for Jessie, intending to pull her into his arms. As he extended his hand toward her, Hurst's usually good nature snapped. This stranger had caused enough stress in his household for one night.

Lunging, he caught Brad's left wrist firmly in his mouth. Brad hollered hoarsely as Hurst's powerful jaws clamped tightly and resolutely around his arm.

"Hurst, no!" Jessie's scream was shrill as she grabbed Hurst's collar.

He released Brad's arm but refused to step away, growling discontentedly as Jessie rolled up the sleeve of Brad's shirt to survey the damage.

"Oh, Brad. I'm so sorry. He's never done anything like this before. I'll get some ice."

"I'm OK. The skin's barely broken." Brad's voice was shaky. "Maybe I should just go to my room now."

"Oh, yes, of course." Jessie was overwhelmed with embarrassment and remorse. "Follow me."

As they headed out of the kitchen, Hurst was right on their heels.

"Maybe the mutt would like to stay here?" Brad looked at the dog with contempt.

"Oh, yes, of course," Jessie mumbled again. "Hurst, stay."

He stopped obediently, looking plaintively at Jessie, and whining.

As she silently led the way to the guest room, Jessie took hold of Brad's right hand.

"The bathroom is right across the hall from you. If you need anything at all, please let me know.

"Brad, I'm flattered that you came all this way to be with me for Thanksgiving. I'm sorry about the dog. I can't believe he did such a thing. I'm sure it was because you frightened us so when you first got here. I feel terrible about it."

Brad's humor was returning. "Jessie, you're babbling. I'm gonna be just fine. Get a good night's sleep, and I'll see you in the morning. I love you, Jess."

Jessie looked at her feet then back into Brad's eyes.

"Yes, we need to get some sleep. And, Brad . . . he's had all his shots."

10

·····

*T*HANKSGIVING DAY DAWNED GLORI-
OUSLY. Thick, wet snow clung valiantly to branches and
housetops, sparkling like fine crystal in the bright sun.

Gram, as usual, was up and around before Jessie. But this
morning Jessie wasn't far behind. Gram sat at the kitchen table with her Bible and her coffee before her and Hurst at her
feet when Jessie barreled into the room.

"You're not going to believe what happened last night!"

"Well, if it has to do with the handsome young man
sleeping in the guest room, you have my undivided attention,
darling."

"That's Brad." Jessie's voice, though lowered to escape de-
tection from the rest of the house, was intense and filled with
emotion. "I didn't know he was coming. He just showed up
here last night to surprise me."

"Apparently he was successful." Gram's smirk belied her
amusement.

"Gram, what are we going to do?"

"We? What are *we* going to do about what exactly?"

"About dinner with Spence and his mother."

"I'm sure one more won't matter. But I'll call this morning
to be sure. How does that sound?"

"We have no choice, I suppose." Jessie rubbed her forehead worriedly. "This has the makings of a disaster."

Gram opened a drawer under the wall phone that hung
in the kitchen and pulled out her address book.

70

"Jessie, I think the number is in here. Look for me, won't you? I know that number; I just can't think of it. Read it to me, and I'll dial."

She lifted the receiver and watched Jessie expectantly.

Jessie obliged, then sat down to listen to Gram's end of the conversation.

"Good morning, Spence. This is Jessica Sterling, may I speak to your mother? . . . Oh, yes, dear, we're still coming . . ." Gram rolled her eyes conspiratorially at Jessie. "Cecilia? Good morning. This is Jessica. I'm fine, dear, looking forward to seeing you in a few hours. Cecilia, we've had an unexpected visitor arrive here late last night, and we were hoping it wouldn't be too much of an imposition if we brought one more guest to dinner today."

Jessie, her elbows on the table, tapped her chin as she watched Gram stand in silence with the phone to her ear as Mrs. McCord answered.

"Thank you so much. I was sure you'd say that. I do so hope it doesn't put you to more trouble. . . . Why, actually I don't believe it's anyone you know; it's a friend of Jessie's from Long Beach. . . . Yes, dear, about 2:00. See you then."

Gram replaced the receiver. "There, that's that."

"Easy for you to say," Jessie grumbled in mock irritation. "I expect my life to start passing before my eyes any minute now."

"Well, look on the bright side, dear. We have someone to drive us out to the farm now. The roads may not be completely cleared by early afternoon."

"Gram, I don't think Brad's ever been out of southern California. This could be the first snow he's ever seen. I imagine you're still stuck with me for a driver."

"Did I hear my name?" Brad cheerfully made his entrance. "Good morning, Mrs. Sterling. I'm Bradley Donnelly." He looked down suspiciously as Hurst came from under the table and sat squarely between him and Gram.

"Welcome, Bradley. I'm delighted to meet you." Then gruffly, "Hurst, get out of the way, I must shake this young man's hand." She pushed Hurst aside with the side of her leg.

Brad's handshake was somewhat tentative as he watched the big dog from the corner of his eye, but Hurst made no move toward him. Rather, he stationed himself at Jessie's side.

Brad turned his attention to Jessie. "Morning, Jess."

"Good morning, Brad. How's your wrist?"

"A little sore, but it's OK."

"What happened to your wrist?" Gram moved in for a look as Brad rolled up his sleeve.

"Hurst bit him last night, Gram. I couldn't believe it. Hurst has never done such a thing."

Gram and Jessie huddled around Brad. Jessie held his left arm lightly in her hand and gingerly touched his wrist. Brad's shirt and sweater had protected his skin from being torn by the dog's teeth, but Hurst's powerful jaws clamped tightly around his wrist had left it swollen and bruised.

"Oh, Brad, it looks terrible." Jessie was contrite. "I'm so sorry."

"We'll ask our family doctor to take a look at it when we get to the farm," Gram added. "He'll know if there's anything we should do. I can assure you, though, Brad, that Hurst has had all the required immunizations."

"So I heard." His irritation was so well masked that only Jessie detected it. "I don't think we need to have anyone else look at it, Mrs. Sterling. I'm a doctor, too, you know."

Gram was undaunted. "All the same, we'll be out at the farm anyway, and I'll feel much better if Spence tells me there's nothing to worry about."

Brad's eyes sought Jessie's in exasperation. Jessie smiled, shrugging her shoulders slightly. She knew Gram's mind was made up. Spence would examine the wrist.

"How about some coffee, children?" Gram asked cheerfully. "Brad, tell me, have you ever seen a more beautiful morning? Just look at that snow."

Brad walked to the window over the sink. "Looks mighty cold to me, and I bet the roads are bad. I guess we won't be able to get off the place today."

"Nonsense. We're used to this kind of weather. Jessie can get us there. Can't you, dear?"

Jessie smiled weakly and nodded. "Brad, get your coffee and come with me. I'll show you the rest of the house."

* * *

The drive into the country was without incident. The bright Thanksgiving morning sun and the traffic had practically cleared the highway. Even so, Jessie drove, because Brad didn't want to take any chances of running into icy patches. As Jessie had suspected, he had no experience driving in the snow.

The small farm home looked warm and inviting, nestled inside a white fence at the end of a long gravel drive. Jessie parked close to the gate and was glad to see that the sidewalk leading up to the porch had been shoveled clean. A covered porch ran the length of the house. The porch swing hung right up next to the ceiling, all slack taken out of the chain for its winter rest. Brightly colored metal lawn chairs—some red, some green—sat idly through these cold months as they had each winter for years, waiting for spring's warmth to bring forth the kindly old woman and her friends, who spent many summer evenings discussing their lengthening pasts and shortening futures.

As the trio waited on the porch for someone to answer the door, Jessie looked out across the fields, thinking that this was the sight Spence had seen every morning of his life until he had gone away to college. She thought of the little boy who had run down the steps of this porch and all the way into town, trying to get help for his injured father.

The door opening behind her interrupted Jessie's thoughts and she turned, expecting to see Mrs. McCord or Spence. Instead it was a woman—a very pretty young woman —on the other side of the storm door.

"Why, Nicole! I didn't expect to see you here." Jessie was surprised but also pleased.

"Hi, Jessie. I'm so glad to see you. Spence was kind enough to think that the baby and I might be alone today, and he called yesterday to see if we would like to come out for Thanksgiving. I was very grateful he did."

A curious heaviness settled in the pit of Jessie's stomach. Just then, Spence walked into the room. His eyes lit up when he saw Jessie.

"There you are—we've been anxious for you to get here." Some of the merriment was replaced with puzzlement as his eyes were drawn to Brad.

"Spence, this is a friend of mine from Long Beach. He surprised us with a visit last night. Your mother graciously insisted we bring him along today."

"Yes, of course," Spence stepped toward Brad, his right hand extended. "I'm Spencer McCord."

Brad grasped Spence's hand and the two shook vigorously. "Bradley Donnelly. Nice to meet ya."

"Likewise," Spence smiled agreeably, then turned to Gram. "Mrs. Sterling, how are you today? Feeling OK?"

"Yes, dear, I'm feeling wonderful. What a lovely day, don't you think? Is your mother in the kitchen? I'll see if she needs some help." Not waiting for any answers, Gram hurried off to the back of the house to find her old friend.

"I'm coming too Mrs. Sterling." Nicole called after Gram. "I need to make myself useful."

Jessie looked from Brad to Spence as the three stood smiling silently at one another.

"Well, I guess I should help out in the kitchen too, if the two of you can entertain each other," Jessie ventured.

"Sure, doll. Spence and I can manage. And if he's as hungry as I am, we need all the hands in the kitchen we can muster. Right, Spence?"

"Quite."

Jessie thought Spence's voice sounded somewhat cool, and she smiled at him nervously as she stepped back two steps and then turned toward the kitchen. But his face was the picture of composure as he nodded agreeably.

If he's upset about Brad, he isn't letting on, Jessie thought as she walked away. And, what about Nicole? What's she doing here? As much as Jessie liked her, a nagging jealousy tugged. Spence hadn't known yesterday that Brad would be here, so he couldn't have been trying to one-up Jessie. Spence didn't seem the type to play games like that, anyway. So what was going on? A worried frown creased Jessie's brow as she joined the other women in the kitchen.

"Something wrong, Jessie?" Nicole seemed genuinely concerned.

"No, nothing." Jessie was brought back from her thoughts. "I was just thinking. Now, what can I do to help?"

*   *   *

Mrs. McCord had prepared a traditional Thanksgiving meal. The turkey sat in front of Spence at the head of the table. His mother was across from him at the other end of the table, with Jessie and Brad to his right and Nicole and Gram to his left.

"I'm counting on you to do the honors by carving the turkey, son," Mrs. McCord smiled at her son.

Spence was congenial. "I rather suspected as much. But first, let's bless the food. Shall we join hands and bow our heads?"

Our Heavenly Father, thank You for the day You've given us, and thank You for each one gathered here. Lord, on this Thanksgiving Day, we acknowledge our losses. I ask for Your special touch on Nikki, Gram, and Jessie. Please flood their hearts with the peace that only You can give. Thank You for bringing this guest across the country safely. Lord, if anyone among us doesn't know You as their Savior, reveal yourself in a personal way. Thank You for sacrificing Christ on the Cross to secure eternal life for Your children. Now we ask Your blessing on this day and on this food. In the name of Jesus Christ, we pray. Amen.

Jessie stole a glance around the table during Spence's prayer. Each one, even Brad, had their eyes tightly shut. Did they all feel something she didn't? She was glad to be here, but to say she was enraptured with gratitude to God was a lie. Surely God didn't expect much from her in the midst of her turmoil. Her life was spinning out of control—she couldn't shake the desire to see Charles suffer, the paper was on the brink of disaster, she was confused about Spence and Brad, and now Nicole seemed to be in the picture somehow. Still, watching Nicole praying across the table as she clasped Spence's and Gram's hands and lifted her face toward heaven, Jessie saw joy in her countenance. She felt a burning within to experience what Nicole felt.

With Spence's *Amen*, everyone looked up toward Spence. He picked up the carving knife and large fork.

"Well, let's start with you, Nikki, white meat or dark?"

Jessie watched as he served her. There was an easiness in the way they related to one another. But just last weekend she had been with Spence herself and had been sure there was a spark between them. Could she have been so wrong?

Brad reached over and covered her hand with his. "Penny for your thoughts."

"I'm afraid you'd be overpaying." Jessie laughed.

"So," Brad addressed the table in general, "I guess I'm the only one here who doesn't know everybody."

"No, that's not true, Brad," Nicole responded. "I've only just met Jessie this week." Sweetly, she addressed Jessie. "But I've got a feeling we're going to be good friends."

In spite of her confusion about Nicole's relationship with Spence, Jessie hoped that they could be friends.

Mrs. McCord and Gram were chatting easily at their end of the table . . . about church, the weather, their health.

"So, Spence, what kind of practice you got going out here?" Brad asked.

"I'm the proverbial family doctor, Brad. That's been my dream since I was a kid."

"Yeah, I've wanted to be a doctor most of my life too. But I'm specializing in allergies. I think that's where the money is. The patients never die, but they never get well. They just come in every week and hand over 50 bucks for their shots." Brad laughed conspiratorially and nudged Jessie's arm with his elbow. "Right, Jess?"

"I guess I hadn't quite thought of it that way."

"Well, you better start thinkin' about it, little lady. If you play your cards right, you might cash in on some of my affluence."

Mortified, Jessie looked quickly at Spence. Their eyes

met, and Jessie was certain he could detect her embarrassment. She felt perhaps he was swallowing the urge to laugh at her predicament.

"Jessie," he said kindly, "may I interest you in white or dark meat?"

"Well, I think that's the wonderful thing about medicine, don't you?" Nicole was sincere. "There are so many different ways you can serve mankind. It's just a question of finding what's right for you . . . Jessie, do you enjoy your work?"

"Why, yes, I enjoyed it very much at the university newspaper in California. But I wasn't prepared for all the headaches in actually running a paper. I'm not sure I've paid my dues long enough and absorbed enough knowledge to be able to handle it the way Dad would have wanted. What about you, Nicole? I don't remember Gram saying if you work outside the home . . ."

"Well, I'm qualified to teach elementary music. But I'm not teaching now. I plan to stay at home with my son until he's old enough to start school."

Brad joined in. "Oh, so you're married then?"

Nicole lowered her eyes. "Well, no. I lost my husband several months ago."

"Lost him?" Brad looked up, interested. "So you're divorced?"

"Carl died," Spence interjected.

"Oh, I'm sorry. You've had it pretty tough."

"It's all right, Brad. I should have just said my husband died. Those words are still hard to get out."

"Where is your little boy, Nicole?" Jessie asked in an effort to change the subject.

"He's here, but he's sleeping. He's only 18 months old so he still naps. He's quite a boy. I can't wait for you to meet him."

"As a matter of fact, Jessie," Spence added, "he's my namesake—Joshua *Spencer* Clark. But we call him Josh."

"*Your* namesake?" Jessie was really puzzled now.

"Yes, Spence and Carl were friends all their lives. Carl grew up right down the road a couple of miles. Both his parents are with the Lord too. Spence is the closest thing I have to family in this part of the country."

"Sounds like a shoo-in to me, Buddy," Brad winked at Spence and nudged Jessie again with his elbow.

"Mother, you've outdone yourself again." Spence pointedly did not respond to Brad's remark.

"Thank you, son. There's plenty, so everyone help yourself. We have three pies—keep that in mind." It was clear Mrs. McCord loved to cook for her friends and loved ones. Living alone, she was probably afraid she was losing her touch, Jessie thought, but she certainly could be proud of the way this meal had turned out.

"Are you sure there's plenty, Cecelia?" Gram asked.

"Absolutely certain, Jessica . . . why?"

"Well, I thought I might take some leftovers home to Phil and Lynn. I can't imagine why they're not here by now."

Stunned silence fell over the group. Nicole gasped ever so slightly, then stared at her plate. Brad looked from face to face to see if anyone else found it amusing. Mrs. McCord, near tears, looked at Spence.

Jessie stared at Nicole's face across the table, not even seeing her. She swallowed the scream that was forming in her throat.

Spence stood, and, with his arm around Jessie's shoulders, pulled her to her feet.

"Mother, Jessie and I will bring the pies in. Will you help me, Jess?" Her knees trembling, she took his hand, and he led her from the room.

11
•••••

BRAD WANTED TO SEE BOSTON. Considering the letters in her mother's closet, Jessie couldn't think of anywhere she'd like to go less. But he was her guest for the holiday weekend, and she would take him. Anyway, she admitted to herself, spending the day sight-seeing with Brad would offer a diversion from the uncomfortable discussions they were bound to have if they remained idle at the house. Since his arrival, Brad had tried every conceivable tactic to ensure her return to California. Jessie was growing impatient with his manipulating ways.

This morning, over breakfast, he was at his most charming. "These muffins are great," he said to Gram as he reached for his third. "How about another one? They don't cook like this where I come from. Maybe you can give Jessie some lessons before we're married."

Gram arched one eyebrow in her granddaughter's direction. "That's interesting, Brad. Jessie learned how to make these muffins when she was a little girl. Maybe you need to persuade her to spend more time in the kitchen."

There was a polite edge in Gram's voice. Even she recognized that Brad's charm wore thin, Jessie thought. He had always seemed so funny and harmless when they were in California. But here in the warmth of her hometown, among her family and friends, he seemed shallow and self-serving.

Jessie knew Gram was watching to see how she would respond to Brad's comment. "I didn't realize we had decided to be married, Brad," she said coolly.

He was immediately contrite. "I know I'm getting ahead of things a little, doll. I haven't even had time to buy you a ring. But under the circumstances . . . with your parents' death . . . and while I'm here . . . I thought your grandmother should be the first to know."

Jessie pushed her chair back from the table with such force that Hurst, who had been lying under it, gave a startled yelp. Before Brad or Gram could react, the only reminder of Jessie's presence in the kitchen was the furious swinging of the cafe doors leading into the living room.

Brad looked at Gram. "Uh, you can see we haven't quite worked out all the details. It's nothing to worry about. Jessie's a little temperamental."

"Nonsense," Gram said, patting Brad's hand. "Jessica is not at all temperamental. She never has been. Now, would you like raspberry jam or orange marmalade on that muffin?"

Up in her room, Jessie angrily packed the canvas bag she would take into Boston for the day. A pair of mittens and a wool scarf . . . how could Brad be so presumptuous and insensitive? Her 35-mm camera . . . what had possessed him to say they would be married? The red earmuffs . . . what on earth would Gram think?

Jessie thrust the last item into the bag and sat on the edge of her bed. So Brad wanted to marry her—to make an official announcement. It was a complication she didn't need in her life right now. To be sure, marriage to Brad would have its advantages. His prosperous life-style and his undivided attention would be hers to enjoy. He had never shown the slightest flicker of interest in another woman since they met two years ago.

Jessie could still recall that first meeting vividly. It was in the Emergency Room at the University Hospital. She was there covering a feature story on a team of paramedics. Brad was the resident on duty. After a preliminary examination of an accident victim with minor injuries, he had approached Jessie.

"You must be new around here. I never miss a beautiful face. I'm Dr. Donnelly. Brad Donnelly."

Jessie *was* new in town, and beginning with his introduction, Brad was determined to befriend her. For more than a year Brad and Jessie were friends, and though he pushed for a more committed relationship, she held him at arm's length. Only in the last several months had she allowed the relationship to deepen. He *did* love her—she knew that. Perhaps his behavior during this Thanksgiving weekend was a desperate ploy to keep her. Perhaps he felt her slipping from his grasp.

Brad's anxious voice at her bedroom door interrupted Jessie's musings. "Jess, are you ready? I've got the car warmed up, and Gram sent some goodies for on the road."

"I'm almost ready," Jessie called cheerfully. "Give me a minute."

"Good. I'll be waiting in the car." Through the closed door, Jessie could sense the relief in his voice.

She waited until his footsteps receded down the hallway before she stood from her seat on the bed. Quickly she checked the canvas bag one more time. She'd forgotten the extra roll of film. Retrieving it from her dresser drawer, Jessie tossed it in the bag. She crossed to the door and paused with her hand on the knob. She had a feeling this would be a day to remember.

The drive from New Hampshire to Boston was magnificent. Even Brad, who was proudly indifferent to "all that great outdoors stuff," was impressed. The foliage was a brilliant mix of crimson and gold, interspersed with an occasional evergreen. The scenery provided a natural topic for conversation, and by the time they approached the city, both Brad's and Jessie's tension had eased.

Jessie parked the car at a train station in the suburbs. "Part of the experience is riding the subway," she explained to Brad. "We'll buy our tokens here and take the red line into the heart of Boston."

The subway was a puzzlement to Brad, and Jessie enjoyed his poorly disguised dismay at the numbers and variety of people riding the public transit system. "Is it always like this?" he asked, as he was shoved onto the train in a sandwich of humanity.

"Always." Jessie grinned over her shoulder and made her way to the back of the car. "Stand here and hold this strap," she directed. "Bend your knees a little and you'll be all right."

The pair exited the train at the fourth stop, the Park Street station. From there it was an easy walk to the Freedom Trail, a 1½ mile tour of historic downtown Boston. Brad slipped his hand around Jessie's and bent close to her face as they walked.

"I'm so glad to be here with you, doll."

Jessie's first instinct was to withdraw her gloved hand from his. But as she started to pull it away, she saw the disappointment in his face, so instead she took hold of his arm.

As they continued following the brick sidewalk, Jessie stopped at each interest point to review its historical significance with Brad. At most stops he would read the large placards aloud. Occasionally Jessie would add bits and pieces of information.

Each time Jessie visited Boston, these monuments—the churches, the graveyards, Fanueil Hall—renewed her sense of awe at the price men and women had paid for freedom. This small hamlet was the cradle of liberty. More than 200 years later she was still enjoying the freedom many of its residents had died to purchase.

Brad and Jessie lingered an especially long time in front of the old North Church.

"I've heard of this place all my life," Brad said. "Paul Revere and his lantern were made famous here. 'One if by land and two if by sea.'"

"Actually, it was a clergyman, the sexton of Old North, who placed the lanterns in the steeple," Jessie explained. "His name was Robert Newman, and he lived right across the street from the church. He climbed 190 feet to the steeple to display the two warning lights. If he were caught, it was sure death by firing squad. A great many heroes of the revolution were clergy."

"Why do you know so much about the history of this

city?" Brad asked, slipping his arm around her shoulders. "You sound like a guidebook."

"Mom and Dad loved Boston. We drove in at least twice a year to walk the Freedom Trail." Jessie's voice caught. "Dad said there was nothing like seeing Boston with Mom—she could recite the history of the whole American Revolution."

Brad pulled Jessie close, pressing her head down to his shoulder. "There's nothing like seeing Boston with you, Jess," he whispered into her dark hair. "I love you. Please marry me."

With her eyes closed, she let her head rest on his shoulder. This is how Mom must have felt, Jessie thought. She was touring Boston, the most romantic of cities, with one man, yet she loved another. Lynn had felt a deep fondness for Charles, yet she was desperately in love with Spence.

Spence? Jessie's head shot up off Brad's shoulder. Philip! She meant Philip. Mom was fond of Charles but loved Philip. Jessie's mind was reeling. *And what about Jessie?* Jessie was fond of Brad, but Jessie loved *Spence!*

The knowledge made her weak. When had she begun to love him? At his apartment perhaps, sitting in his well-worn chair. In the church service, as his strong clear voice read the Scripture lesson. At Thanksgiving dinner, when he showed such kindness to Gram. *When* she had begun to love Spencer McCord Jessie didn't know, but she knew this—she loved him, and now no one else would ever do.

"Well, Jess? Jessie, I'm waiting for an answer." Brad's sharp question interrupted Jessie's frantic thoughts.

Jessie looked at him, a little dazed. How would she tell Brad that she couldn't marry him? That she was never in love with him? "Let's talk," she whispered, touching his cheek with her hand.

"Jessie, I don't want to talk." Brad's voice got louder, and Jessie noticed heads turning in their direction. "I've just asked you to marry me. I don't want to talk—I want an answer!" He was shouting now.

"Brad. Lower your voice. You're causing a scene. I just want to talk about things . . . about us." She looped her arm through his and led him toward one of the many historic graveyards dotting the Freedom Trail. They slipped in the gate and walked carefully around the old slate markers. Jessie led Brad to a weathered granite bench and sat down. Huddled together in the cold, the couple looked like any pair of young lovers planning their future.

"Brad ..." Jessie took a deep breath, which was just enough time for Brad to interject.

"Jessie, I'm sorry. I shouldn't have yelled at you that way. It's just that, well, a man doesn't expect to get dead silence when he asks a woman to marry him. Maybe it was the wrong time . . . or the wrong place . . ."

Or the wrong person, Jessie thought, looking sadly at Brad. She hated to hurt him like this.

"I'm not in love with you, Brad." Jessie spoke the words as softly and kindly as she knew how. "I care about you. And I love you—in a way. But not in the way it takes to make a marriage."

Jessie looked steadily at Brad as she spoke. She knew he was searching her eyes for any hint of indecision. She must be sure he found none.

"Jessie, you don't mean that." She could tell he didn't believe his own words. "The last few weeks have been too hard on you . . . And besides, if you don't love me, you will. You can learn to love me. I'll make you love me. Please, Jess . . ." Brad's voice choked.

Jessie felt her resolve start to weaken. She must not give in. Yet, Brad had been so good to her . . .

"Jessie, we're meant for each other." Brad had regained his composure. "Anyone who sees us together knows that. We deserve the good life. We've earned it. Marry me and come to California. You want more than a little hometown paper can ever give you."

Brad's cajoling renewed Jessie's determination to see this through. She took his hand as she spoke.

"Brad, you don't *love me*—not really. You love what I can do for you. And you're more upset that you can't have your way than that you can't have me."

"You're wrong." Brad shook his head.

"I'm not who you think I am. You and I are different. The things we want from life are different. I always knew that, Brad. But coming home has shown me the truth of it more clearly than ever before."

"I'm not convinced, Jess. And I'm not giving up. I'll never give up."

Jessie smiled at his stubborn determination. In an odd sort of way, it was part of what endeared him to her. She rose from the bench and stretched out her hand.

"C'mon. It's so cold today you can see your breath—too cold to sit still so long. We've got a lot of Boston left to see."

12

·····

NIGHT HAD FALLEN when Brad and Jessie turned into the long drive in front of Jessie's home. She was tired . . . it had been a trying day. But, she knew she had done the right thing, and she felt good about her honesty with Brad. She knew he loved her in the only way he knew how. And she owed him the truth . . . she owed herself the truth.

They parked around back, and Jessie noticed a visitor's car parked close to the side of the house as they went in through the small back porch. In the dark, she didn't recognize it. As they entered the kitchen, Jessie called out for her grandmother.

"Gram? I'm home."

"Jessie?" It was Spence's voice she heard floating in from the living room. Her heart jumped at the sound of his voice, and she hurried toward the front of the house. But Gram wasn't with him and Jessie suddenly felt uneasy.

"Spence, where's Gram? Is something wrong?"

"No, Jess, everything's OK." Spence reassured her. Brad walked into the room but didn't speak.

"Then, where's Gram?" Jessie's voice was insistent.

"She had an appointment with me this morning. You and Charles had insisted she see me because of the dizzy spell she had earlier this week."

"Yes, I know." Jessie nodded. "She left the house to see you about the same time Brad and I left for Boston this morning. We're just getting back I haven't talked to her since then."

Spence continued. "When she came in this morning, I did the routine things ... took her pulse and blood pressure, listened to her heart. Everything seemed fine. But in view of her dizzy spell and then the memory lapse yesterday, I insisted she check into the hospital for a couple of days."

Jessie looked at him closely. Was he telling the whole story?

"Oh, I should have come with her to your office today. I never dreamed she'd end up in the hospital."

"It's purely a precaution, Jess. I just want to get a CAT scan and do a few other tests ... plus, I think she needs to be forced to stay in bed for 24 hours and get some rest. Each of the symptoms she's been experiencing could be the result of stress—nothing more—but she's up in years, and we need to be sure."

"Well, I'll just clean up a little and then run over to the hospital." Jessie started toward the stairs.

"Oh, no you don't." Spence was firm. "She's resting now. I told her I'd come to the house and see you personally so you wouldn't feel obligated to go to the hospital to see for yourself. It will serve no purpose for you to go there tonight."

"Are you sure?" Jessie was hesitant. "I don't like for her to be alone."

"She's not alone, Jessie. There are nurses 'round the clock who will take good care of her. She's probably asleep for the night by now."

"Well, I guess you could be right."

"I know I'm right. I'm a doctor." Spence smiled reassuringly into her eyes.

"He's right, Jess." She had forgotten about Brad until he spoke. "We doctors know about these things, and besides, you're probably as tired as I am."

"Did you enjoy Boston?" Spence looked at Brad for the first time.

"It could have gone better," Brad said moodily. "But I can say I've seen Boston now."

Was Jessie imagining it, or did Spence look relieved?

"Well, I'll be going. Promise me you won't leave for the hospital as soon as I'm gone."

Spence and Jessie walked toward the door. They were about to say goodnight when Jessie stopped and looked back at Brad, then back to Spence.

"Spence, are you staying at your apartment or the hospital tonight?"

"I was planning to sleep at home unless I'm called back. Why?"

Jessie shuffled her feet uncomfortably. "Well, it's just that with Gram gone, I don't think it's appropriate for Brad to stay here with me."

"Oh, come on, Jess," Brad was irritated. "I think you're safe with me."

"That's not the point, Brad." This was one argument Spence was glad to take part in. "I'm sure you wouldn't want Jessie to be compromised in anyone's mind."

"I'm sure," Brad mimicked back. "And what's Jessie's reputation to you?" Jessie saw the muscles in Spence's jaw set, and he took a step forward.

"Ah, forget it," Brad pouted. "Let me get my stuff."

Within five minutes the men were gone, and Jessie wearily climbed the stairs to her room. Her mind was too full to think clearly. She didn't turn on the bedroom light but flopped across her bed without undressing. Mentally and physically exhausted, she immediately drifted into a troubled sleep.

* * *

The clanging of the telephone pierced into Jessie's fitful sleep. Confused, she reached for the alarm to turn it off, but the persistent ringing continued. Finally, coming awake, she reached for the phone.

"Hello?"

"Jess, you awake?"

"Oh, hi, Brad. Actually, I wasn't awake, but I should be." Jessie glanced down and realized she was still in yesterday's clothes. "What time is it?"

88

"It's a little after 7:00. Spence suggested I ride to the hospital with him. We'll be headed that way in a few minutes. What time will you be there?"

"I'll probably leave here in about 40 minutes. I should be there by 8:00."

"Spence said to tell you that your grandmother is in room 302. I'll see ya there. OK?"

"OK. It's a good thing you called . . . I didn't intend to sleep this late."

Jessie was anxious to see Gram, yet it was hard to hurry through her morning routine. A heaviness had settled upon her, and she felt sluggish and unrested. On her way out the back door, she noticed Gram's Bible on the kitchen table.

"Oh, I bet she would want this with her," Jessie said aloud. She picked it up and opened it. On the inside of the front cover, Jessie recognized Gram's handwriting . . . *Romans 8:38 and 39.* Curious, Jessie leafed through the pages.

"Let's see . . . I think that's in the New Testament." She turned toward the back. Matthew, Mark, Luke . . . yes, she remembered these books of the Bible from Sunday School days. John, Acts . . . here it is, *Romans 8:* Quickly she turned to verses 38 and 39. *For I am persuaded, that neither death, nor life, nor angels, nor principalities, nor powers, nor things present, nor things to come, Nor height, nor depth, nor any other creature, shall be able to separate us from the love of God, which is in Christ Jesus our Lord.*

That's true for Gram, Jessie thought. Nothing had ever separated her from the love of God . . . not Gramp's death nor the loss of her son and daughter-in-law. Oh well, I don't have time for this. Jessie solemnly closed the book and, clutching it to her, hurried out of the quiet old house.

Gram was sitting up in the hospital bed looking through a magazine when Jessie arrived.

"Jessie, darling. You didn't have to get out so early."

Jessie smiled brightly and held Gram's Bible in front of her with both hands. "Thought you might need this."

"Indeed, I do. Thank you, dear, for bringing it to me.

Now, tell me, how was your day yesterday? Did Brad enjoy Boston?"

"Gram, you're not fooling me," Jessie wagged her finger close to Gram's face and chuckled. "You're not the least bit concerned about what Brad thinks of Boston; you're interested in what Jessie thinks of Brad."

"All right, I admit it. That young man is thinking about marriage. What are you thinking about?"

"Well, not about marriage." Jessie's face was serious now as she sat down on the edge of Gram's bed. "I was really glad to see him when he arrived the other night . . . I guess I had missed him more than I realized. And I'll miss him when he leaves. But I can't give him what he wants . . . and that's commitment. Although he's dear to me, I'm not in love with him. Not the way Mom was with Dad or the way you were with Gramps."

"Did you tell him that?"

"Yes. But Brad's mind is not easily changed. He's going back today, though . . . alone. I think he was determined to take me back to California with him when he arrived. So I made some progress. I don't want to hurt him, Gram."

"You're a sweet girl, Jessie. In your entire life, you have never wanted to hurt anyone. If you told him the truth, that's all you can do. I don't believe Brad is God's best for you, dear. Be patient."

"I didn't come here to talk about me. I came here to see about you. I would have come last night, but Spence wouldn't hear of it. How are you feeling this morning?"

"I'm feeling quite well, to tell you the truth. Much too well to be in the hospital. Spence did a few tests yesterday, and it seems that physically I'm fine. He thinks I'm suffering from the stress of the last few weeks. Wants me to take better care of myself—typical doctor stuff, you know."

"Well, I'm going to see to it that you do just that. You gave me such a scare." Jessie put her arms around Gram's shoulders and the two women embraced. "I'm going to take good care of you."

As Jessie pulled away from Gram and stood up, Spence came into the room.

"And how are the two Jessica Sterlings this morning?"

"One of us is beautiful and one of us is old. Which do you think is which?" Gram looked at Spence with mock grouchiness.

"I think you're both beautiful, and I think you're pulling our leg about your age, Mrs. Sterling. The results from yesterday's tests tell me I'm dealing with a lady in good physical condition. I'm going to keep you in here one more night, just for good measure, then you can go home tomorrow afternoon. How does that sound?" Spence glanced from Gram to Jessie and back to Gram.

"Spence is right, Gram. Stay one more night just to be safe. OK?"

"Well, I suppose." Gram was not pleased at the prospect. "Let me talk to Spence alone a moment, won't you, dear?"

"Of course, I'll be right outside if you need me."

Jessie left Gram's room and looked up and down the hall for Brad but didn't see him. She remembered that there was a waiting area by the elevators on each floor, so she headed in that direction.

As she had expected, Brad was sitting on a sofa in the waiting area. He stood when he saw her coming. Jessie's heart flinched a little at the sight of him. For one second she thought how comforting it would be to walk into his arms and ask him to take over her life. How she yearned for someone to carry this burden. But she knew that, in fairness to Brad, she must not reopen even a crack the door she closed yesterday.

"Hi, Jess." He searched her face as he greeted her. Jessie knew what he was hoping to see in her eyes.

Even before she said hello, she noticed his suitcase on the floor close to where he had been sitting.

"So, you're all ready to go. Can I drive you to the airport?" Her throat was constricted, and her smile was weak.

"No, thanks, I've arranged for a cab." Brad's voice wasn't angry, just flat and purposely void of emotion.

"I could stay, Jess, if you need me. I mean, with your grandmother in the hospital and all."

Jessie pressed her fingers against his lips to quiet him. "No, Brad. I need to handle this myself. There's really nothing you could do. I think it's best if you go."

Brad took her hand from his lips and held it against his cheek. Their faces only inches apart, he looked deeply into her eyes.

"This isn't the end, Jess. I'm not givin' up this easily." His lips brushed hers as he spoke, and his arms slid tightly around her waist as he pulled her against him.

She clung to him, knowing there would be a void in her when he was gone. Oh, Brad, she cried silently, I'm so sorry. I wish you happiness and love.

Suddenly he backed away from her. The elevator doors swung open, and he quickly picked up his bag, stepped inside, and turned to face her. She swallowed the desire to speak his name and call him back into her life.

As the heavy doors closed between them, Brad mouthed, "I love you." Jessie dropped her head and whispered, "Goodbye, Brad." Slowly she turned toward Gram's room.

"Jessie, may I speak to you for a moment?" Spence's voice startled her. How much had he seen?

"Yes, of course. What is it?"

"It's about your grandmother. Come sit down with me a moment." Spence motioned to the sofa in the waiting area.

Jessie moved toward it quickly, her eyes focused on Spence's face. "Please tell me, Spence. You're frightening me."

"There's no need to be frightened. Your grandmother is in fine shape physically. But over the next few weeks I want to run some tests. Unfortunately, Jessie, what I suspect as the problem can ultimately be very serious."

Jessie tensed and her voice was sharp. "What, Spence? What do you suspect?"

"I think there's a possibility your grandmother is in the early stages of Alzheimer's disease."

Jessie stared at him, frozen. As the enormity of his words

began to sink in, Jessie felt herself falling apart. "It can't be. Not Gram. Oh, Spence . . ."

His arm was around her now, and with his hand he pushed her hair back from her face and spoke soothingly.

"Jessie, listen to me. It's going to be all right." His voice was strong and reassuring, and Jessie took comfort in his presence and his touch.

Calming, she asked softly, "What will this mean for Gram?"

"It's only a suspicion, Jessie. It's not a diagnosis. I hope I'm wrong. This particular disease takes a long time to pinpoint. And, even if I'm right, she has some good years ahead of her. It usually progresses slowly, and there could be weeks or months between incidents like the one out at the farm on Thanksgiving." Seeing the despair on Jessie's face, Spence's voice softened even more, "This probably wasn't the right time to bring it up. It was stupid of me to upset you like this."

"Forgive me for falling apart like that, won't you? Of course you had to tell me." Jessie was pulling herself together. "The possibility of Gram leaning on me instead of the other way around just hadn't crossed my mind. Suddenly I feel so afraid . . . so alone."

Her eyes searched Spence's face, but the voice she heard was behind her. "You're not alone, Jessica. As long as I'm alive, you're not alone."

"Charles! How long have you been standing there?" Jessie was on her feet now, embarrassed that Charles might have seen her in a moment of weakness. Spence rose from the couch also, and he and Charles shook hands.

"I heard," was all that Charles offered. "Jessie, Gram is not just your responsibility. She's my mother, and I love her. If Spence is correct in his suspicion, we'll take care of her together. You needn't feel alone. We'll work our way through this."

"Oh, really, Charles," Jessie's composure snapped. "I don't want your help. Haven't you done enough?" Jessie could hear her own voice—it sounded as though someone's hands were around her throat—and she couldn't stop herself. "And Gram wouldn't want your help either, if she knew what I know."

Jessie could see the open-mouthed disbelief on his face. But still she didn't stop.

"I found the letters you wrote my mother before she and Dad were married. I know how you felt about her. But you couldn't have her, could you? She loved your brother instead. So you made him pay, didn't you, by forcing him out of Gramp's paper. Tell me, when you were driving my father to an early grave, did you ever dream you were going to kill my mother too? Or did you expect to have her to yourself?"

Jessie was close to him now, spitting the accusations without reserve. "Well, can't you think of anything charming and Christian to say, Charles? Or do you want to remind me again of how I'll never be alone as long as you live?"

Charles' face was ashen. "No, Jessie, I don't have anything to say. I had no idea you felt this way. If I had known, I could have—I would have—I'll talk to you about this later, Jessie." Quickly he turned and hurried away from her down the corridor.

She stared after him, sobbing, her fist to her mouth.

"Come with me, Jessie." She had forgotten Spence was there. "Let's go into my office. You can have some privacy there. I'll stay with you until you're feeling better." His arm firmly around her waist, they started to his office.

"Thank you," were the only words that would come. She wanted to tell him so much more. She'd lost count of the times he had held her together during the last few weeks. She wanted to tell him she was in love with him and that she thought she had seen something in his eyes that made her think he might love her too. But there's Nicole, she reminded herself. And Nicole is the kind of girl he would want—sweet and joyful. Jessie couldn't even remember feeling joy. It seemed like this confusion and bitterness had plagued her forever. Her life was in shambles. Mom and Dad were gone, the paper was on the brink of disaster, and now Gram was sick.

No, she had nothing to offer a man like Spencer McCord.

13

•••••

*I*T WAS LATE AFTERNOON when Jessie returned home from the hospital. She had spent most of the day in the room with Gram. Maybe this was all some terrible mistake—this Alzheimer's business—Gram had seemed quite well today. Cheerful—not at all forgetful or uncooperative. Herself. Gram had seemed herself. Spence wasn't sure, he'd said. As a matter of fact, it was virtually impossible to be sure. As Jessie moved in the kitchen, preparing her evening meal, she almost audibly voiced these thoughts. She wasn't really talking out loud to herself, rather whispering, her lips barely moving, her countenance worried and intense.

She ate alone at the kitchen table, Hurst at her feet, his chin resting on his front paws. Occasionally Jessie scratched behind his ear with a slippered foot. He didn't acknowledge her affection as he enjoyed it, but sighed loudly when she moved her foot away. Jessie was grateful for his companionship tonight. Her mood was nervous and unsettled, pierced with fearful thoughts of the future—the paper's, Gram's, and her own.

After eating and quickly washing and putting away her few dishes, Jessie's thoughts turned to the remainder of the evening. She was too agitated to sit quietly and watch television or read. So she wandered aimlessly from room to room, much as she had a few days after the funeral. But now, rather than a prisoner of overwhelming grief and loneliness, she was the unprepared, unwitting guardian of the lives of others. It would be she who would see Gram through whatever medical tests Spence had in mind over the next few weeks. It was she whose decisions, right or wrong, would affect the lives of the faithful employees of Dad's paper, and it was she who had forced a change in Brad's well-laid plans and sent him back to California alone.

Jessie found herself in her dad's study on the first floor and settled into his easy chair, her feet on the hassock in front of her, her head laid back, staring at the ceiling. Hurst flopped noisily onto the hardwood floor beside the chair, and Jessie unconsciously let her hand float down to the top of his head, her forefinger moving back and forth quietly in the thick red fur.

Jessie replayed her verbal assault on Charles in her mind. Some of her hatred, strangely, had dissipated with the smoke of the bullets she had hurled at him. He had looked so wounded. But there was no way he was completely innocent, Jessie reminded herself. Jessie's thoughts vacillated between considering the remote chance that she was wrong about Charles to patting herself on the back for being the only one who could see through him so clearly. Suddenly the chilling thought of Gram finding out what she had said to Charles clutched her. Gram would be so angry with Jessie if she knew. No matter what he had done, Charles was Gram's son. Jessie mentally calculated the chances of Gram finding out. Spence wouldn't tell her, she was sure of that. And Charles was not likely to open this particular can of worms with Gram. So it was improbable, Jessie decided with a relieved nod of her head, that Gram would ever hear of it.

Jessie's thoughts turned to Spence. Her realization of her feelings for him yesterday when she was in Boston with Brad were really only the awakening of a sleeping emotion within her since the day she met him. And Jessie had been so sure his feelings were the same—and Gram had seen it too. "How could I have misjudged him so completely?" she asked herself aloud. She shrugged and shook her head. Oh, she hadn't misjudged him as a person—he was sensitive, dedicated to God and mankind, thoughtful, considerate—Jessie smiled ruefully at her own use of the Boy Scout cliches—certainly unbefitting a journalist.

But what, Jessie tapped her fingers on the arm of Dad's chair, was his relationship with Nicole? She cocked her head and pursed her lips. I could just ask him, she thought. Jessie's recent verbal boldness with Brad and then Charles had served to bolster her confidence in direct communication. A self-imposed assertiveness training course, of sorts. Quickly she thrust the idea from her. No, if such a conversation made Spence uncomfortable and embarrassed, it could very well stiffen their friendship—and having him for a friend was almost as important to Jessie as having his romantic attention.

Jessie was surprised by her own lack of jealousy toward Nicole. There's just nothing bad to say about her, she admitted silently. If she is the woman Spence loves, I can't say that I blame him. And although several feminine subtleties that might be useful in winning a man's affection came to mind, Jessie's good sense told her that they would be wasted on a man like Spencer McCord.

Slowly, Jessie's face reflected a knowing that welled up from within her. She wouldn't try to convince Spence to love her, she wouldn't try to outdo Nicole for his affection—and the reason was very simple. She trusted him. Her respect for his wisdom and his instincts was so solid that she knew he would make the right decisions for the three of them—himself, Nicole, and Jessie. If he loved Nicole, so be it. Jessie would be their friend, and she would not put her own desires ahead of their relationship. She knew it was the right decision. It was good to have this inner peace about at least one of the burdens weighing on her slender shoulders.

The room had grown quite dark as Jessie sat mentally pilfering through her life. She flipped on the light next to Dad's chair and got up to start a fire. She stacked a few logs onto the grate and wadded up some newspaper to stuff under them to light. As she worked at the hearth, Jessie thought about one thing Spence and Nicole had in their lives that she envied. Not their relationship with each other—real or imagined—but their relationships with God. That had to be the key to their contentment. Gram had it too. How did one get it? She thought briefly of getting a Bible from the bookshelf and looking through it. But she wouldn't know where to start and, even in her solitude, felt a little embarrassed to go fumbling through the Bible for answers when she wasn't even sure what the questions were.

Jessie brought forth a long fireplace match from its decorative box and struck it. She touched it to the newspaper and waited expectantly as the flames spread slowly through the newspaper and began to lick at the logs. She got on her knees before it and began to blow vigorously at the flames as she had seen her father do a hundred times before. Predictably, the logs began to catch and the well-aged wood popped and cracked as the flames lifted themselves lustily toward the chimney.

Melancholy swept over Jessie as she sat on her knees before the fire. But she pushed it aside with the practicality that survived within her troubled spirit. There would be no time for self-pity and clinging to the past. Jessie's life—and Gram's —would be in her hands now. Jessie knew, as she pushed herself to her feet, that the only help she could possibly count on would have to come from the God that sustained Spence and Nicole and Gram. Even Charles seems to know God better than I do, she thought resignedly.

She went to the bookshelf and pulled out a paperback Bible. It didn't have the substantial look of Spence's leather Bible or Gram's. Could words of knowledge and wisdom be found in a Bible with paper binding? Even in her spiritual state, Jessie felt God's Word to be deserving of something more dignified. That's silly, she reprimanded herself. God's Word is God's Word. She returned to Dad's chair and sat with the unopened book on her lap.

"Well, God," Jessie's voice cut through the silence of the firelit room. "I could use some of Your wisdom. If You would be willing to guide me like You seem to guide others, I would be willing to follow You."

That said, Jessie relaxed back into Dad's chair. She wasn't sure whether to expect any insight at this point or not. So she sat quietly, hearing only the cracking fire and the occasional stirrings of Hurst as he shifted positions at her feet.

Jessie didn't know at what point she nodded off, but the sound of tires on the gravel driveway roused her. The house was dark except for the floorlamp by the chair where she sat, and as Jessie made her way to the front of the house, she turned on the lights, flooding the living room and entry hall with light. By the time she reached the front door she heard the closing of a car door and her visitor's steps crossing the porch. Jessie turned on the porch light, and a voice reached her from the other side of the heavy oak door.

"Jessie? It's Charles."

She groaned inwardly, but her features were masked by cold indifference as she swung open the door.

"May I come in, Jessie? I'd like to talk to you."

Jessie hesitated—how simple it would be to merely close the door on this unpleasantness. But her inherent kindness wouldn't allow her to slam the door in his face, so she grimly nodded her consent and stepped aside for him to enter.

There was a short awkward silence, then Jessie spoke.

"Well, Charles, what is it you want to talk to me about?"

"Jessie, I've been distressed all day—after what you said at the hospital this morning. I was hoping we could straighten it out."

"Come into the living room." Jessie led the way. She was surprised at her lack of desire to belabor the points she had assailed him with earlier in the day. It was as if the words she had hurled at him at the hospital had punctured the balloon of hatred she carried in her heart for him. Now, she simply wanted not to see him or talk to him.

Barely into the living room, Charles waded into the conversation.

"Jessie, what you said at the hospital . . . we need to talk about it. There's been some misunderstanding—I loved your parents, and I can't see how you think I had a part in their deaths. Please tell me where you got that idea."

Jessie looked at him for several seconds—the prolonged silence hung tensely in the air. When she spoke, her voice was measured and controlled.

"A day or two after the funeral, I was in my mother's

closet looking through her things. I found some old shoe boxes containing photographs, important papers, letters, things of that sort. There were some letters addressed to her in Boston, and the return address on the envelopes was this house. I assumed they were from my father. They were from you, Charles. Letters—love letters—from you to my mother. I had always been curious about you, you know. We never saw a lot of you. It seemed to me that you and Dad should have been closer, being twins. I wondered why you didn't have a family of your own and why you didn't spend more time with us. I wondered why Dad left Grandpa's paper and you stayed. When I found those letters, it seemed to answer my questions. You hated my dad because he married my mother—and you were in love with her."

Charles' eyes had never left her face as she spoke. "Jessie, honey, I wish you had come to me immediately when you found those letters. I could have saved you so much unpleasantness. To tell you the truth, it never occurred to me that Lynn might have kept them."

Jessie had been standing in front of the sofa, and Charles stood near her. She sank into the end of the sofa and tucked her feet under her now—an invitation for Charles to sit down also and tell her the rest of the story.

He sat down in the large chair facing her and continued.

"Yes, I loved your mother. But she saw something in me that I hadn't seen in myself. She knew from the start that I wasn't the kind of man to marry and raise a family and do the routine things that are expected of a good husband and father. She told me just that in her last letter to me. She'd met Phil while she and I were seeing each other, and it was clear to her that he was what she wanted—and just as clear that I wasn't. I was a man driven by my work—the paper. It was, and still is, my first love. As a matter of fact, I met another woman a couple of years after your mother. She sent me packing for the same reason. It took some time for me to see that they were both right."

Jessie lifted her eyes defiantly to meet his. "Then why did you hate Dad so? Why did you and Grandpa squeeze him out of the business?"

"Jessie, I loved my brother, and I don't believe he ever even hinted to you that we ran him out of the business. I can't imagine where you got that idea. He wanted out—he wanted a slower pace, more time with his family. I knew it wasn't going well for him the past few years. As a matter of fact, we were negotiating to merge his operation into mine. I even guaranteed him I would keep all his people—he was concerned about them being out of work if he folded. Where did you get the idea we squeezed him out?"

She looked at her lap where her hands lay, clenched together. Not accustomed to being at a loss for words, her stammering sounded foreign to her ears. "Well, I . . . I guess . . . I guess I got the idea somewhere. I suppose I assumed it."

She looked at him then, expecting a show of anger. Her cheeks reddened as she thought of the things she had said to Gram and Spence.

Charles rose from the chair and came and seated himself next to her on the couch. He took both her hands in his. Jessie couldn't bring herself to meet his gaze, and he gently lifted her face toward him until their eyes met.

"Jessie, I had no idea you felt this way. I didn't stay away because of the thing with your mother . . . or because I didn't love my brother; I was just a self-centered, thoughtless bachelor, running my business and not giving a thought to whether or not I was hurting anyone else. Can you find it in your heart to forgive me for that? I want to try to make it up to you. Will you forgive me?"

Jessie was stunned. She had made terrible accusations against this man—a man everyone knew to be a good Christian man. Everyone but her. And he was asking *her* to forgive *him*.

"Yes, of course. There's really not anything to forgive you for. I guess I was wrong. I was terribly wrong." Jessie knew it was she who should be seeking forgiveness, but she couldn't humble herself to ask. Even though she knew he would grant it, she couldn't find the words.

Charles rose. Jessie was dumb with embarrassment as she

stood to see him to the door, but her pride wouldn't allow her to reveal her remorse.

"Well, then," Charles seemed somewhat at a loss as to how to end their conversation. "Would you like for me to bring Mother home from the hospital tomorrow?"

"Oh, no thank you," Jessie was holding the door open for him. "She's expecting me to be there early in the afternoon. But, thank you for asking."

Charles had one foot out the door when he hesitated and turned back to her.

"Jessie, I want you to know, the offer I made your father to buy his paper still stands. And I would retain all his employees. However, if you are determined to keep it, I will do anything I can to help you make a success of it. You think it over—I want you to know you're not trapped with the paper. Spence mentioned that he thought you probably wanted to return to California as soon as possible. Although I'd personally like to see you stay here, selling the paper to me would certainly give you more freedom. You think about it, and if you're interested, we'll talk about it in more detail. Goodnight."

Jessie closed the door behind him and leaned against it. Hot tears stung her eyelids. Could she have been so wrong? What must Gram think of her? And Spence? Someday maybe she could bring herself to tell them that she'd made a terrible mistake.

She made her way back to Dad's study. The fire was smoldering now, and she decided to let it burn out. This long, draining day had come to an end.

What was it in a man that prompted him to ask forgiveness because she had been foolish enough to misconstrue his behavior? She should have known when Spence defended him that Charles was not what she thought. And Gram . . . Gram must have been crushed by Jessie's hatred for Charles. Yet she never accused Jessie or rebuked her.

"What kind of person am I, anyway?" she spoke aloud to herself as she climbed the stairs in the silent old house. "What kind of person am I?"

14

•••••

JESSIE PAUSED A LONG TIME in front of the arched door to the old stone church. Finally, she grasped the circular iron handle and gave it a hefty jerk. She winced at the grating of the heavy door on the stone steps as it swung open. Inside the sanctuary several heads turned at the sound—the service had started 15 minutes ago.

Jessie slipped into a pew on the back row. She almost hadn't come this morning. She knew Gram would inquire—and yet, that really didn't play into her decision. Something else, a familiar ache within her, a sense of loss and longing, drew her to this place.

Nicole was at the pipe organ, and Jessie watched her at the keyboard. Nicole and Spence would be happy together, she decided. The resolution she'd made last night to step out of the race for his affection seemed right to her. In fact, it seemed like the only right thing she'd done in the last few weeks. Nevertheless, loneliness gnawed at her emotions as she watched Nicole. They would make a fine family—Spence, Nicole, and little Joshua. But had Nicole ever felt the way Jessie did when Spence held her those few moments that snowy winter evening at Gram's? The memory of his overcoat against her cheek and his breath in her hair brought hot tears to Jessie's eyes.

Never mind, Jessie told herself firmly. I've got Gram to think about. And I won't interfere.

As the congregation stood to sing from the hymnal Jessie's eyes swept over the crowd. Spence wasn't there. She couldn't find Charles either.

Charles. How courageous of him to come to see her last night. Given similar circumstances, Jessie wasn't sure she would have done it. As she recalled their conversation, her face flamed red. She had been wrong about Charles. And worse than that, she had accused him and defamed him to both Spence and Gram. Her wrath was unwarranted and inexcusable. She hadn't really tried to find the truth, jumping from one unsubstantiated conclusion to another. She could hardly believe it when he asked for *her* forgiveness. For some reason, she couldn't bring herself to reciprocate, even though she knew her fault was greater than his. Jessie's heart was softened toward Charles, but she knew she hadn't completely resolved her animosity.

As Jessie reflected on this, the service was progressing in a very unextraordinary way. She couldn't remember who read the Scripture passage or what it was about. Nevertheless, something was working in her heart. A change was being wrought.

Jessie's thoughts turned to Gram. What a precious relationship the two had shared over the years. Gram, who had always been there for Jessie, strong and . . . what was the word Gram had used to describe Spence? Unwavering. In their character, Gram and Spence were alike; strong and unwavering. Jessie couldn't bear the thought of life without Gram.

Would Spence's suspicions be correct? Jessie tried to imagine Gram without her dancing eyes and quick wit, but she couldn't do it. Would Gram become a shell of a person like so many of the Alzheimer's victims Brad had described to her and poked fun at? And if she did, how would Jessie find the strength to be to Gram the kind of support Gram had always been to her?

Dropping her head to her chest, Jessie sat quietly. She was at the end of herself. Gram. Jessie loved her so much. Silent tears slid softly down her cheeks. She knew she was unequipped to handle what lay ahead. A deep repentance welled up within her.

The service concluded; Nicole played the postlude; the

parishioners filed by Jessie unnoticed. She sat perfectly still in the last pew. Finally, she opened her eyes and was surprised to see that, save Nicole, the church was empty. Jessie grasped the red hymnal she had been holding in her lap and set it beside her. Quickly she rose from her seat and headed toward the front of the church. As Jessie reached the steps leading to the chancel she paused. Dropping to her knees, she lowered her head on the red-carpeted stairs and began to pray.

In a moment Nicole was there, her arm around Jessie's shoulders. Nicole never spoke, but Jessie could feel her trembling and realized Nicole was weeping. The two women stayed on the stairs until a nursery worker brought Joshua Spencer through the side door of the sanctuary. When he saw his mother, the toddler gave a little shriek and started toward her in a teetering run. Lunging for Nicole, at the last minute Joshua veered off course. He landed directly in Jessie's lap. Laughing through her tears, she gently righted him. Nicole was laughing too, and she and Jessie embraced quickly before they parted.

Jessie's mind was blessedly clear as she walked across the parking lot toward the car. The brilliant autumn sunshine had long since melted last week's snow. The pin oaks and soft maples sheltering the church were still beautiful, but past their peak. Winter would soon be settling in.

Jessie paused for a moment, stretched her neck back, and let her head rest on her shoulders. The brisk fresh air filled her lungs, and she exhaled a long, contented sigh.

"Exhilarating, isn't it?" The voice came out of nowhere. Suddenly Spence was beside her, and the intensity of his presence made her gasp. She stared at him mutely.

"Did I startle you?" He clasped Jessie's elbow lightly and began steering her toward her car.

"Yes . . . no . . . I mean . . . I didn't know you were here today, that's all."

Spence laughed as he watched her. "That's because I arrived near the end of the service. I snuck in the vestibule. I promised Nicole I'd spend some time with Joshua today. He misses his daddy." He paused. "Sorry I interrupted you a minute ago. You seemed lost in thought."

"I was just enjoying the last remnants of autumn." Jessie gestured at the trees in the direction they were headed. "Isn't it beautiful, Spence? Winter will be here too soon."

They were at the car now, but Spence seemed in no hurry to leave. He stood leaning with one hand on her car, and she gazed at the woods beyond them as she listened to him speak.

"I think winter is my favorite season," he said slowly. "It's true, the beauty of autumn fades. And for some people, that process represents death and dying. For me . . . maybe because I'm a doctor . . . that's not so. I've always thought of winter as a season of glorious change. A time when things are working that we can't see. Winter gives me hope. In the winter I know it's only a season till spring."

Jessie turned her eyes from the scenery to look at Spence.

"That's just like my life," she whispered.

Surprise flickered across Spence's face, and his eyes pierced hers. In a moment his hands were on her shoulders, pulling her tight against him. She felt his lips crush her mouth and his arms so tight about her she couldn't breathe. She couldn't move out of his embrace . . . she wouldn't.

Just as suddenly as the kiss had begun, it ended. He released her, and she stood limply against the car. His face was fierce with a series of emotions she couldn't read.

"I'm sorry, Jessie. I shouldn't have done that," he said hoarsely. Without a word he turned and started back across the parking lot.

* * *

Jessie was hardly aware that she was driving to the hospital. The sensation of Spence's lips on hers lingered. The force of his kiss had surprised her, and the memory of it made her weak even now. But her mind was in turmoil. Clearly, his attraction to her had not been her imagination. What should she do? Jessie had vowed not to interfere in Spence's relationship with Nicole. Surely Nicole loved him—what woman

106

wouldn't? And little Joshua should have a daddy—Spence had practically said so. Yet, could Jessie live here, in such a small town, with the man she loved but could never have? Should she stay here, secretly hoping and believing that he loved her too?

Jessie wheeled recklessly into the hospital parking lot and stopped the car. What should she do to make things bearable for the three of them? She walked through the glass doors of the hospital lobby and headed for the elevator. Maybe she should go away for a while. "Five, please," she said to the nurse's aide nearest the control panel on the crowded elevator. That was the best idea. She'd go away—to California. Gram would be able to take care of herself with Charles' help. She stepped off the elevator in front of the waiting area on the fifth floor. Could she go back to California without going back to Brad? Yes, it was over between them.

Jessie's preoccupation came to an abrupt halt as she started down the corridor to Gram's room. A flurry of activity at the end of the hall caused Jessie to break into a controlled run. Three nurses were restraining someone in a doorway—someone that looked very much like Gram. As Jessie approached, one of the nurses caught sight of her.

"Here comes her granddaughter!" The nurse was speaking to the two women helping her and then to Jessie, "Miss Sterling, hurry. Can you help us please?"

Gram was fighting two nurses with her arms and kicking the third. When she saw Jessie, her struggle intensified.

"Jessie! They've taken my clothes. They've hidden my clothes, and they won't tell me where. Let go of me!" Gram's shriek became a plaintive whimper. "Jessie, make them let go . . . please make them let go."

Gram stopped struggling and hung her head. The nurses cautiously released her, and Jessie gathered the older woman into her arms. "I'm here, Gram. It's OK . . . I've come to take you home."

Jessie guided Gram into her room and into a sitting position on the bed. She went quickly to the closet and retrieved

Gram's clothes, bringing them to her and laying them in her lap.

"See, Gram, they weren't hiding your clothes," she said gently.

Biting her lip, Gram looked at Jessie and whispered, "I'm sorry. It's just that I asked that nurse when I could go home, and she said she didn't know. I wanted to put my clothes on . . . she said, 'Not yet.' I thought they wanted to keep me here. I got so angry . . . I'm afraid, Jessie." Gram's voice choked. "And I'm so ashamed."

"Let's go home now," Jessie said softly, beginning to help Gram into her clothes. "That is, if you're feeling up to it?"

"Up to it? Of course I'm up to it." Gram's voice was getting firm. "I've been waiting all morning. Oh yes, that reminds me . . . Jessica, you *did* go to church today?"

15

.....

CALIFORNIA WAS OUT OF THE QUES-
TION. After Gram's episode at the hospital, Jessie had given
up the idea completely. The most she could hope for was that
the terrible stress of the last months had temporarily caused
Gram to lose her ability to cope. The possibility that her condition was something more serious would only be revealed in
time. Jessie hated the waiting and the uncertainty.

Most days, Gram acted normally. Occasionally she would
have minor lapses, and often Jessie couldn't tell if they were
legitimate symptoms or merely the manifestation of old age.
As she reflected on Gram's condition, Jessie recalled several
incidents in the last weeks, but could not assess their significance. For instance, when Jessie and Charles sat at the kitchen
table reviewing Dad's books and Gram excused herself because she "never did understand these business matters."
Gram had managed Grandpa's books for years. Was her statement a not-so-subtle effort to get Charles and Jessie to com-
municate, or was she trying to disguise the fact that she
couldn't work with numbers any more? Jessie just didn't know.

She had similar questions about the episode when Gram
couldn't remember Cecilia McCord's telephone number, one
she had dialed frequently for years. Another peculiarity was
that Gram knew Nicole Clark's husband was dead but
couldn't remember why. As the days passed and November
melted into December, Jessie often watched and pondered
Gram's behavior. Was Gram just growing old or was Gram
sick?

Jessie longed for Spence terribly during these weeks.
Many times she had suppressed the desire to telephone him

and inquire about something Gram had said or done. Instead she wrote her questions in a small notebook and kept them safely in her nightstand. There would be time enough for questions at Gram's next scheduled appointment. She would not risk any action, however small, that Spence might misconstrue as an excuse to talk with him.

He had apologized for kissing her. "I shouldn't have done that," he had said. The words played in Jessie's mind over and over again. He probably felt that he had betrayed Nicole. Jessie must never let him know how much she loved him. If she was committed to live with Gram and be so near Spence as a result, she would have to trust God to heal her wounded heart.

Jessie saw Spence periodically, usually at church. He was always kind to her, but she sensed him keeping a certain distance between them. Several Sundays Jessie noticed him carrying Joshua to Nicole's car. Obviously, the little boy adored him. Jessie's heart ached each time she saw the three together, but knowing she had made the right decision comforted her.

For her own mental health, Jessie immersed herself in a feverish attempt to see what could be done with *The Courier.* She was headed there this morning, the backseat of her car loaded with the boxed 5-foot artificial Christmas tree and the accompanying decorations Dad had displayed in the office every year as long as she could remember.

As the car bounced over the winding country road and her cargo clattered behind her, Jessie considered the coming holiday. Last year she spent Christmas with Brad. She'd worked in the newsroom until late Christmas Eve. He met her there, purposely leaving his pager at home; they met some friends and went caroling. Afterward, there was a party, and Brad had given her a lovely watch. It was fun—but Jessie distinctly remembered wishing she were home celebrating quietly with Mom and Dad. The memories of Brad evoked Jessie's affection, but she had no desire to see him. How much had changed in one year. This holiday would be a quiet one all right, celebrated without Mom and Dad for the first time in her life.

Christmas at Dad's newspaper wouldn't be the same either. She would continue his traditions, just the way he would have wanted her to. She would plan the party, make the Christmas cake, sign the bonus checks. For all Dad's employees and faithful friends, life must go on.

Jessie was surprised to see Charles' car as she turned into the parking lot of *The Courier.* She glanced at her watch—only 7 A.M. What would he be doing here this time of morning? As she pushed open the big front door to the newsroom, and it banged shut behind her, she looked quickly for Charles. He was sitting on the corner of Lacy Thompson's desk, eating a doughnut and drinking a cup of coffee.

"Morning, Jess! You really ought to fix that door."

To her surprise, Jessie was glad to see him. It would be the first real contact she'd had with him since the night he'd come to see her.

She grinned. "I know. But that's the way Dad liked it. He called it the doorbell."

"Sounds like Philip," Charles agreed affectionately. "Lacy and I were just talking about the time he closed the office for a week so that the staff could vacation between Christmas and New Year's Day."

Lacy shook her head. "That Thursday, half the town called complaining their paper hadn't been delivered."

Jessie laughed. It felt good to reminisce about Dad. It felt good to know that Charles loved him too.

"Do you have a minute?" Charles asked Jessie, motioning to Dad's office.

Pouring a cup of coffee, Jessie gestured toward the door. "Surely. Come in and sit down."

Jessie led the way and, acutely aware of all the curious eyes and ears in the newsroom, shut the door carefully behind her.

Charles settled himself comfortably in one of the old tattered chairs, but Jessie didn't give him a chance to speak.

"I'm glad you came, Uncle Charles. I've been wanting to tell you . . . I've been wanting to tell you I'm sorry. I misjudged you, and I was terribly wrong in the way I acted." Jessie's voice quavered. "I'm sorry, Uncle Charles. Will you forgive me?"

"Forgive you?" Charles voice boomed through the small office as he moved to hug Jessie. "You jumped to some very understandable conclusions, that's all. And of course I forgive you."

"Thanks." As Jessie whispered the reply she knew the issue was finally settled in her heart.

"You've had a hard go of it lately, honey," Charles said tenderly, pushing back a wisp of her hair. "That's why I came today. Will you hear me out?"

Jessie nodded gratefully and sank into the chair behind the old oak desk.

Uncle Charles cleared his throat noisily. "Frankly, Jessie, I need you. Your skills are invaluable to me. My managing editor, who happens to be my best feature writer, is leaving to go to a larger daily. No one on my staff is strong enough to fill that spot. I've interviewed more than five outside applicants." Charles paused and leaned across the desk. "Jessie, I want you. You're the only person I know who can do the job the way it needs to be done."

Work for Charles? Jessie had never contemplated the possibility. Yet, what once would have repulsed her now seemed worth considering. She sat thoughtfully, weighing the offer.

"Now, I know what you're thinking," Charles continued hastily. "I have all the details worked out. We won't forget *The Courier*. I'll buy it—it's an institution in this town, you know. We'll market it to all my subscribers as a weekly supplement to the daily paper they already receive. The boost in subscriptions will shore up the finances. If we can't meet our budget, I'll subsidize it."

"What about the staff?"

"Jessie, the staff can stay. Of course they can stay. They've run this paper for years . . . and, honey, I don't want to sound unkind . . . but they don't need you to do it."

Jessie nodded soberly. "I know. But Charles, *why* are you doing this? You said you needed *me*, but there has to be more to it . . . Is it for Dad?"

Charles paused and Jessie waited. "It *is* for Philip, Jessie. And for all those years we wasted. But it's more than that. It's because for years I was too busy to notice what *The Courier* means to this town. It's our identity piece. It provides the strand of continuity that holds our community together. When you read *The Courier* you read about your friends and neighbors. My daily, even though its headquartered here, can't do that—it covers the whole region. We can't let *The Courier* die, Jessie."

Jessie's eyes searched Charles' face. "What did Dad think?"

Charles looked at her earnestly. "He agreed, Jess. We had already talked strategy on the new subscription campaign. I was supposed to schedule an appointment to draw up the papers the day of the accident." He hesitated. "I've wanted to talk in detail with you about this many times, but your grandmother said it was too soon and . . . well . . ."

"And I wasn't very approachable," Jessie finished. She smiled. "Well, it looks like I don't have much of a decision to make. Dad made it for me." She rose from her seat behind the desk and stretched out her hand.

"Uncle Charles, you've got a deal."

16
•••••

 B Y MID-DECEMBER, Jessie had settled comfortably into her new life with Gram and working for Charles at his paper. As Christmas approached, she looked forward to the holiday, even though she knew she would be longing for her parents. But this year, the meaning of the season was fresh and joyous—the birth of Christ the Savior. She and Gram were determined to make the day memorable and had invited Charles, Mrs. McCord, Spence, Nicole, and Joshua to their home for dinner. Jessie knew most of the responsibility for Christmas dinner would rest on her shoulders, and she was not experienced in the preparation of big holiday dinners. But she felt the diversion would help her through what would otherwise be a lonely day.

Jessie was surprised and pleased when Nicole called the Saturday before Christmas and asked if she would like to go shopping in the afternoon and then go out for an early dinner. One of the teenage girls from the youth group at church had called Nicole and offered to baby-sit with Joshua so that she could have some time to shop for him. Except for church and work, Jessie had hardly been out of the house since Gram had been released from the hospital, so she was pleased for the opportunity.

The two young women chatted and laughed as they shopped for special toys for Joshua. Jessie picked up a few small items for Gram and found a book she thought Uncle Charles might enjoy. By the time they arrived at the restaurant, they welcomed the chance to sit down and relax. After thoroughly examining the menu, both women ordered Boston scrod then settled into comfortable conversation.

"I'm really looking forward to spending Christmas Day with you, Jessie." Nicole's sincerity was reflected in her smile. "Just like Thanksgiving, I was dreading being alone, and a dear friend saved the day for me."

"Gram and I feel the same," Jessie offered. "We know there will be some painful moments, but it will be easier for us having all of you there."

"My parents wanted me to come there for Christmas. They're retired in Florida, but I know if I go, they'll pressure me to stay. With Carl gone now, they think Joshua and I should move in with them. To tell the truth, it's an idea I'm seriously considering."

Jessie's eyes widened in surprise, and before she could think better of it, she blurted out, "But what about Spence? I'm sure he wouldn't hear of having you that far away."

Nicole shrugged nonchalantly. "Actually, he thinks it's not such a bad idea. He says a sense of family and history could be a good environment for Josh, since he isn't going to have his father."

"But Nicole," Jessie couldn't believe it was she who was attempting to talk Nicole out of this notion, "it would be very difficult for you and Spence to maintain a long-distance romance. You'd hardly see each other."

Nicole sat staring at Jessie as if she couldn't quite comprehend what she was hearing. Suddenly, as Jessie's words sunk in, amusement tugged at the corners of her eyes and mouth.

"Romance? *Romance?* Whatever made you think Spencer and I had a romance to maintain?" Nicole giggled as she looked expectantly at Jessie.

"Well, you seem so close, and you're together quite often. He's so fond of the baby . . . and of you, too, of course. It just appeared to me that the two of you were involved."

Nicole shook her head emphatically. "Well, you were wrong. I love Spencer, but only as a dear friend. He and Carl were very close. He sort of took us under his wing after Carl died. But I can assure you that he has no romantic interest in me, and I have none in him."

It took only a moment for hope to reach full bloom in Jessie's heart. Spencer McCord was not in love with Nicole Clark. It didn't occur to Jessie at that moment that he had not professed love for her either. She only knew that he was not going to someday marry Nicole.

Just then, the waiter brought their salads. Jessie thanked him profusely and cheerfully turned her attention to her salad. Nicole watched her curiously. If she noticed that her dinner companion was suddenly more animated and gregarious, she politely did not comment.

* * *

Jessie was disappointed when she didn't see Spence in church the next morning. She was so anxious for him to appear that she found it difficult to concentrate on the sermon—a problem she hadn't experienced since the morning she put her life into God's hands.

Spence was still foremost in her mind Monday morning when she reported to the paper for work. But Charles had given Jessie tremendous responsibilities in her new position, and the stress of the workday quickly drove her thoughts to the tasks at hand. She was wrapping up a meeting with the feature staff when the receptionist reported that Charles wanted to see her upstairs. Jessie glanced at her watch—11:00 already! She'd better hurry. Charles would be leaving for lunch soon. Jessie promptly left the copy desk and opted to take the stairs up the two flights to Charles' office rather than wait for the elevator.

"Jessie! Come in, honey." Uncle Charles met her at his door with a hearty hug. "Working hard?"

As Jessie sank into the overstuffed chair in the plush office, she gave an exaggerated sigh. "You certainly know how to keep a girl busy, Uncle Charles. I haven't stopped since I hit the door this morning."

Uncle Charles perched himself on the edge of his desk. "I

told you I needed you," he said grinning. "Have you had time to miss *The Courier* yet?"

For an instant, a look of melancholy swept across Jessie's countenance. "Maybe a little," she confessed softly.

"And rightly so." Uncle Charles was nodding his head. "I imagine they're missing you too, Jess. And your dad." He looked at her quizzically. "In case you have forgotten, today is Christmas Eve."

Jessie smiled, and Uncle Charles continued.

"Mrs. Thompson, Jim Perry, Joe . . . they will be needing their bonus checks. I'd appreciate it if you'd deliver them. And spend the afternoon there if you'd like. Their Christmas party won't be the same without you." Charles moved to the chair behind his large executive desk.

Gratefully, and with a new respect for Charles, Jessie agreed. He had just handed her the checks when his secretary, Mrs. Adams, buzzed him on the intercom. Jessie could not hear her end of the conversation, but Charles instructed her to "send him right in."

"I'd better run if you have a visitor," Jessie offered and started to rise to her feet.

"No, honey, that's not necessary. You know this visitor. It's Spence. We're going to lunch—he's here to pick me up."

Jessie looked toward the door as it opened, and Spence entered the room. He seemed surprised to see her.

"Why, Jessie, I didn't expect to find you here. How are you?" He walked over to where she was sitting. Jessie didn't notice that Spence hadn't acknowledged Charles who was sitting behind his desk, a welcoming smile on his face.

"I'm doing well, Spence. Didn't Uncle Charles tell you I'm working for him now?"

"No—he just told me he had bought your father's paper. I assumed you sold it so you would be free to return to California."

The look in Spence's eyes as he watched her, the tone in his voice as he spoke, sharpened her senses. Attempting to remain calm, her body nonetheless tensed, and she was unaware that she was clutching the leather arm of the chair as she straightened.

Charles' smile was frozen as he sat ignored, shifting his eyes from one face to the other. He made no attempt to speak to Spence.

"I expect Brad is very unhappy that this job will delay your return," Spence said intensely. No trace of cordiality could be found on his face. His eyes were fixed on Jessie's.

"Brad isn't expecting me to return to California." Jessie's heart began to pound. "I told Brad it was over between us when he was here at Thanksgiving."

"You did?" Spence was incredulous. "When he spent the night at my apartment, he said you'd be returning to California to marry him as soon as you could get your affairs here in order. Why would he tell me that?" Spence looked at her, expecting an answer.

Jessie smiled brightly and rose to her feet. "He probably assumed he would change my mind."

"And I assumed he was telling the truth." Spence was smiling too.

"Well . . ." Jessie looked down at her feet briefly before meeting his gaze. "I assumed you were in love with Nicole."

Charles, assuming his presence was no longer required, slipped quietly through the door, closing it behind him.

Spence laughed loudly, throwing his head back. He opened his arms, pulling Jessie to him and holding her close.

"I'm in love with you, Jessie. I have been since the day I first saw you. I should never have given up—I should have told you."

Jessie relaxed into his arms, absorbing his closeness and the feel of his cheek against hers. Their tears of joy mingled as they clung to one another.

"You're telling me now, Spence. That's all that matters. I thought there was no chance for us." Jessie's voice was husky with emotion. "I love you."

Spence took her shoulders in his hands and held her away from him, looking deeply into her green eyes. "Well, I won't chance losing you again. Will you marry me, Jessie? Will you be my wife?"

Jessie threw her arms around his neck. "Yes! Yes!" His arms around her waist, he lifted her off her feet and swung her around.

Then his mouth was on hers. Her heart soared as he held her, tenderly at first, then his arms hardened as he pulled her against him urgently. His lips brushed her cheeks, then her hair, and he whispered gruffly, "Oh, Jessie, I love you . . . I love you . . ."

In unspoken agreement they drew apart, their hands clasped together between them.

"How long must I wait to make you my wife?" Raising her hands to his lips he added, "Personally I don't believe in long engagements, do you?"

"Not anymore." Jessie laughed as she spoke. "How about the spring. Let's have a spring wedding."

"Perfect." Spence nodded in agreement. "You must be reading my mind. What a glorious winter we'll have . . . planning our life together . . . and spring isn't far away."

"Spring," Jessie murmured through tears as she lifted her face to his. "It's only a season till spring."

Uncle Charles opened the door and started into the room, then stopped as he saw the couple, their arms around one another, their lips touching tenderly. Smiling broadly, he backed out of his office once again, pulling the door shut.

"Mrs. Adams, call Jack Stanley in billing and see if he's free for lunch, will you please? Tell him I'll meet him in the parking lot."